DAVID HAF

JOHN BUNYAN'S
A PILGRIM'S PROGRESS
IN EVERYDAY ENGLISH

A 16TH CENTURY CLASSIC
IN 21ST CENTURY LANGUAGE

ISBN: 9798873999002

PUBLISHED BY THRIVE! BOOKS

TABLE OF CONTENTS

About the Author

What people are saying…

The Pilgrim's Progress in Everyday English

 Faith Builder

☆☆☆☆☆ **Very readable.**

Reviewed in the United States on December 26, 2023

A lot has changed in the last 350 years, but not Bunyan's message. An excellent read.

Mere Christianity in Everyday English

 Mr. Jerry W. Gammon

☆☆☆☆☆ **Make Lewis Come Alive**

Reviewed in the United States on December 28, 2023

Verified Purchase

If you love C.S. Lewis but have a difficult time understanding some of his archaic language, you need this modern English version by David Harrison. Mr. Harrison takes the language of mid-twentieth century England and gives it an update making Lewis more understandable and enjoyable to the modern reader. A great read.

 thomas klema

☆☆☆☆☆ **Profound**

Reviewed in the United States on February 19, 2024

Verified Purchase

Plumb the depths of the reasons for the Christian faith. I have given this book as a gift to many people searching for truth. It never disappoints.

 Monty

☆☆☆☆☆ **Finally!**

Reviewed in the United States on March 1, 2024

Verified Purchase

I am so impressed Mr. Harrison has done what I wish had been done before. He took a marvelous work that, for some folks, like myself, can be lost in the language used in some parts of the book. Lewis' Mere Christianity & The Screwtape Letters have a profound message that people like myself can get a better understanding by rewording parts in a more modern vernacular that can be absorbed deeper both mentally and spiritually.
Thank you Mr. David Harrison. Well done sir !

THE SCREWTAPE LETTERS IN EVERYDAY ENGLISH

 Penelope Zelasko

☆☆☆☆☆ **Great alternative to the original**

Reviewed in the United States on March 7, 2024

Verified Purchase

I didn't realize this existed until I started searching. I purchased a Screwtape letters by CS Lewis, but found the British language difficult to read. David Harrison is a genius and making things come to life when your culture is very and you can't understand the original.

 Kindle Customer

☆☆☆☆☆ **C S Lewis is always amazing**

Reviewed in the United States on January 11, 2024

Verified Purchase

I ordered two so my husband and I could read together. The language is easier to read than C S Lewis's first editions. Quick delivery.

DAVID HARRISON was born and raised in England and emigrated to Canada in 1973 at the age of 21.

When he was 35, David became a Christ-follower. He is married and the father of two adult children. He attended a Brethren Bible Chapel in Scarborough for 25-years, ten of those years as an elder.

For 23-years David ran an audiovisual integration company in Toronto, Canada, catering primarily to universities, banks, and law firms.

In 2006 David founded Bus Stop Bible Studies[1], a ministry which used public transit advertising panels to display messages of encouragement from the Word of God to many millions of people in Canada.

For 10-years David served as Board Chair of Daystar Native Christian Outreach, based on Manitoulin Island.

Now 'retired', David and his wife, Wendy, run a bed & Breakfast in Muskoka, and David (who failed miserably in English at school) has taken to writing as a hobby.

Contact: dohauthor@gmail.com

---

[1] bit.ly/BSBSIMAGINE

Joseph Middleton
1784

THE
Pilgrim's Progress
FROM
THIS WORLD,
TO
That which is to come:

Delivered under the Similitude of a

DREAM

Wherein is Discovered,
The manner of his setting out,
His Dangerous Journey; And safe
Arrival at the Desired Countrey.

I have used Similitudes, Hof. 12. 10.

By *John Bunyan.*

Licensed and Entred according to Order.

LONDON,
Printed for *Nath. Ponder* at the *Peacock*
in the *Poultrey* near *Cornhil,* 1678.

INTRODUCTION AND THE LIFE OF JOHN BUNYAN

When I read *MERE CHRISTIANITY* for the first time, I was left wondering if the average North American reader would be able to follow along without having an English-to-'English' dictionary at their side. Even I had to Google the meaning of some of Lewis' 1940's colloquialisms. Lewis himself makes reference to the changes in language and word usage over time.

This led me to rework the book into *MERE CHRISTIANITY IN EVERYDAY ENGLISH*. Never did I expect such a positive response to my efforts, with a seventy-nine percent five-star rating on Amazon.

Now, if the English language can change so significantly in the seventy-plus years since Lewis wrote many of his books, imagine how much the language has changed in the 360 years, or so, since Bunyan wrote *THE PILGRIM'S PROGRESS*. Does anyone know what a 'slough', 'tinker' or 'similitude' is?

If you have previously read the original *THE PILGRIM'S PROGRESS*, you will notice that some of the characters' names have been changed. This has been done so that Bunyan's original intent, each character's name having significance, has been honoured. For instance, Mr. By-ends has been changed to Mr. Easylife, Timorous to Fearful, and so on.

John Bunyan's life is a fascinating story of transformation and dedication. Born in 1628 in Elstow, near Bedford, England, he initially had only a basic education before joining the Parliamentary Army at sixteen during the English Civil War. His early experiences in the army were formative, but it was his return to civilian life that set the stage for his most significant contributions.

After the army, Bunyan became a tinker[2], a trade he learned from his father. His life took a spiritual turn following his marriage. He became deeply involved in religion, first attending the parish church and then joining a nonconformist[3] group in Bedford. His commitment to his beliefs was profound, and he soon became a preacher, a role that would define much of his life.

The restoration of the monarchy in England brought challenges for nonconformists like Bunyan. His refusal to stop preaching led to his arrest and a twelve-year imprisonment. Remarkably, it was during this difficult period that Bunyan's literary talents flourished. He wrote *GRACE ABOUNDING TO THE CHIEF OF SINNERS*, a spiritual autobiography, and began work on

---

[2] Tinker—a person who travels from place-to-place mending metal utensils as a way of making a living.

[3] Interestingly, my first cousin twelve times removed, Nicholas Ridley, Bishop of London, in 1548, helped Cranmer compile the first Book of Common Prayer. Nicholas Ridley was one of the first nonconformists, individuals who were Protestant Christians but did not 'conform' to the governance and usages of the state church. Ridley and Cranmer were burned at the stake, hand-in-hand, May 27, 1596, on the orders of Queen Mary, for being heretics. DH

THE PILGRIM'S PROGRESS, which would become Bunyan's most famous work and a significant literary and religious text.

Bunyan faced imprisonment again in 1676 when Charles II withdrew his Act of Indulgence. However, this second imprisonment lasted only six months, during which he completed THE PILGRIM'S PROGRESS.

Some have expressed concern over Bunyan's references to the character, Pope, in this story. It should be noted that Bunyan wrote the Pilgrim's Progress in the years following the *Roman Inquisition*, the *selling of indulgences*, and the *Protestant Reformation*. It is important to understand context in this regard.

The later years of Bunyan's life were more comfortable. He continued to be a popular author and preacher and served as the pastor of the Bedford Meeting. His death at the age of 59 came after falling ill on a journey to London. He was buried in Bunhill Fields, leaving behind a legacy as a prominent figure in Christian literature.

THE PILGRIM'S PROGRESS became one of the most published books in the English language, a testament to Bunyan's enduring influence as a writer and preacher. His life story, marked by adversity, faith, and creativity, remains a source of inspiration and a testament to the power of conviction and perseverance.

Enjoy!

David Harrison

CHAPTER 1 — THE CITY OF DESTRUCTION

While wandering in a wilderness of this world, I found a sheltered place to sleep. That night, I had a vivid dream. In it, I saw a man in ragged clothes, standing a short distance from his house, holding a *Book* and a heavy weight bearing down on him. The man opened the Book, and as he read, he started crying and shaking. Overwhelmed, he cried out, "What shall I do?"

The ragged man went back home, trying his best to hide his distress and anxiety from his family. But he couldn't keep his troubles to himself any longer. Finally, he confessed to his wife and children, "My dear family, I am in deep distress because of this heavy burden I carry. I'm sure that our city will be destroyed by fire from Heaven, and we'll all be ruined unless we find a way to escape."

His family was stunned. They didn't really believe his fears, thinking that he was having a mental breakdown. Evening approached and they hoped sleep would calm him, so they hurriedly put him to bed. But he had a restless night, filled with sighs and tears. In the morning, he said he felt even worse and tried to talk to them again, but they became cold and harsh with him, thinking he was going insane.

Feeling isolated, he spent his time alone, praying for his family and seeking comfort for himself. He walked the streets near his house, sometimes reading, sometimes praying. He continued like this for several days.

In my dream, I saw the man walking in the fields, reading his Book. Still deeply distressed, he cried out again, "How can I be saved?" He looked around, confused and unsure where to go. Then a man named Evangelist approached him and asked, "Why are you crying out?" The troubled man replied, "Sir, this Book tells me I'm condemned to die and face judgment. I don't want that to be my end."

Evangelist asked, "Why don't you want to die, considering all of life's troubles?" The man answered, "I'm scared that the burden I carry will drag me into Hell. I'm not ready for death or judgment. That's why I'm crying out." Evangelist then asked, "If that's how you feel, why don't you move on?" The man said, "I don't know where to go."

Evangelist gave him a scroll that read, *Flee from the wrath to come!* Reading it, the man looked earnestly at Evangelist and asked, "Where should I flee?" Evangelist pointed across a wide plain and asked if the man saw a Narrow Gate or a shining light. The man saw the light. Evangelist advised him to keep the light in sight and head towards it, where he would find the gate and learn what to do next.

In my dream, the ragged man started running towards the light. As he left, his family called for him, pleading for him to return, but he ignored them, focusing only on finding Eternal Life. He ran on, not looking back, heading towards the middle of the plain.

CHAPTER 2 — OBSTINATE AND PLIABLE

As Christian continued his journey (Christian was the ragged man's name), the neighbors came out to see him run. Some mocked him, "Run, Christian, run!" others threatened him, and a few shouted for him to come back. Among them were two men, Obstinate and Pliable, determined to bring him back by force if necessary. They quickly caught up to him.

"What do you want?" Christian asked them. They wanted to persuade him to return. But he couldn't. "You live in the City of Destruction, where I was born too, but if we stay, we'll end up worse than dead in a place of eternal fire! Come with me!" he urged them.

Obstinate was incredulous, "You want us to leave all our friends and creature comforts?" "Yes," replied Christian, "because what we leave behind in this life doesn't begin to compare with what I seek. If you come with me, you'll see it's true." Obstinate kept questioning what he was after, that could cause him to leave everything behind. Christian explained that he sought an unperishable inheritance in Heaven, as described in his Book.

Obstinate dismissed his Book and implored him to return with them. He refused. He was committed to his journey. Obstinate then urged Pliable to leave with him, calling Christian a sucker. Pliable, however, was intrigued by his words and chose to join

Christian. Obstinate, frustrated, decided to return home alone, calling them misled fools.

Pliable asked Christian if he knew the way to this wonderful place. He explained that a man named Evangelist had directed him to a Narrow Gate and seek further instructions.

They set off together.

As they traveled, he expressed his happiness that Pliable had joined him. If Obstinate had understood the powers and terrors of unseen realities, he might not have turned back so quickly. Pliable was curious about the wonders he described to him. He explained they were better comprehended in thought than described in words but offered to tell him more from his Book.

Pliable questioned the truth of his Book. Christian assured him it was written by One who cannot lie. He asked about the glorious things Christian mentioned. He described an eternal kingdom, everlasting life, crowns of glory, shining garments, a place with no sorrow or tears, and the company of angels and redeemed souls, all perfect and immortal.

Pliable was captivated, eager to know how to enjoy these things. He told him they were freely given to those who truly desire them, as recorded in the book. Excited, Pliable suggested we quicken our pace, but Christian was slowed by the burden on his back.

CHAPTER 3 — THE SWAMP OF DESPONDENCY

In my dream, just as Christian and Pliable finished their conversation, they neared a very muddy swamp in the middle of the plain. Not paying attention, they suddenly fell into it. This swamp was called Despondency. There, they struggled, covered in mud. Christian, weighed down by his burden, began to sink deeper.

Pliable cried out in distress, "So, Christian, where are we now?" Christian, equally troubled, admitted, "Honestly, I don't know."

Pliable, frustrated and angry, confronted Christian, "Is this the happiness you spoke of? If we're facing such troubles at the start, what can we expect later? If I manage to get out of here, you can continue to your noble destination alone!" With that, Pliable struggled out  of the swamp on the side closest to his home and left without looking back.

So Christian was left alone in the Swamp of Despondency, struggling towards the side farthest from his home and closest to the Narrow Gate , but he couldn't escape because of the heavy burden on his back.

In my dream, a man named Help approached Christian and asked why he was stuck there. Christian explained, "Evangelist directed me this way to the Narrow Gate to escape the coming wrath. As I hurried, I fell into this swamp."

Help questioned, "Didn't you see the steps?" Christian replied that he hadn't seen them in his hurry. Help offered a hand, pulling Christian out of the swamp and setting him on solid ground, urging him to continue his journey.

Christian, feeling thankful for the assistance received, asked why the swamp hadn't been fixed to ensure a safer passage for those on the pilgrimage. Help clarified that the Swamp of Despondency represented the accumulation of scum and muck that emerges from the fear, doubt, and despair that sin brings to one's conscience. Despite numerous attempts and an abundance of sound advice aimed at remedying its condition, the swamp remained irreparable.

The King's workers had gone to the lengths of installing solid steps through the marshland, yet these steps often went unnoticed or induced a sense of vertigo, which led to many pilgrims losing their footing and tumbling down.

Meanwhile, Pliable had returned home and faced mixed reactions from his neighbors. Some praised his decision to return, others called him a fool for attempting the journey in the first place, while others mocked his cowardice, saying he should have persevered despite the difficulties. Feeling ashamed, Pliable initially kept a low profile, but as he regained his confidence, his neighbors continued to ridicule him behind his back.

Chapter 4 — Mr. Worldly Wiseman

As Christian was walking along the trail, he saw someone in the distance, crossing his path. This person introduced himself as Mr. Worldly Wiseman, who lived in the town of Carnal Policy, not far from his hometown, the City of Destruction. His departure from the City of Destruction had been widely discussed, so Mr. Worldly Wiseman was aware of him. Observing Christian's struggles, he started a conversation.

"Hidey-ho, neighbour, why are you walking with such a heavy load?" Mr. Worldly Wiseman inquired.

"I am heavily burdened, more than anyone can imagine," Christian responded. "And since you've asked, I am on my way to the Narrow Gate ahead. I've been told that there I can learn how to be free from this oppressive load."

"Do you have a family?" Mr. Worldly Wiseman questioned further. "Yes, I do, but this burden is so overwhelming that it's as if I can't even enjoy their company. It's like I don't have a family at all."

"If I give you some advice, will you take it?" asked Mr. Worldly Wiseman. "If your advice is sound, surely I will, I am in dire need of it." Mr. Worldly Wiseman advised, "You must rid yourself of that burden as quickly as possible for peace of mind!"

"That's exactly what I'm seeking," He responded. "I want to be free of this burden, but I can't do it myself, and no one back at home could help. That's why I'm on my way to the Narrow Gate."

"Who told you that was the way to get rid of your burden?" he asked. "An upright and honorable man named Evangelist," replied Christian.

Mr. Worldly Wiseman cursed Evangelist's counsel, warning him of the dangerous path ahead, filled with hardships and possible death, and he couldn't understand why he'd risk his life following a stranger's advice. Christian insisted, "This burden is more dreadful to me than all those dangers! I'll face any risk to be free of it."

Mr. Worldly Wiseman questioned how he got the burden in the first place, and suggested it was from reading the Book. He blamed Christian's confusion and current state on meddling with matters far too complex for him, leading to dangerous choices. Christian firmly stated, "I know what I seek: relief from this burden!"

Mr. Worldly Wiseman then offered an alternative, suggesting a visit to Mr. Legality in the village of Morality. He claimed Legality could remove his burden, and if he didn't want to return to the City of Destruction, Christian could move his family to Morality, a pleasant town with affordable living.

Conflicted, Christian considered his advice, thinking it might be wise to follow Mr. Worldly Wiseman. He asked for directions to Mr. Legality's house. "See that hill?" Mr. Worldly Wiseman pointed out. "Go by that, and the first house is his."

In my dream, I saw Christian turn off the Narrow Path towards Mr. Legality's house. But as he neared the hill, it loomed so large and threatening, with flashes of fire, that he was too scared to continue. His burden felt heavier than ever, and he trembled with fear, regretting that he ever listened to Mr. Worldly Wiseman.

Just then, Evangelist appeared, making him blush with shame. He asked sternly, "What are you doing here, Christian?" He was speechless.

Evangelist continued, "Aren't you the man I found weeping outside the City of Destruction?" "Yes, sir, I am," he replied.

"Didn't I direct you to the Narrow Gate?" he asked. "Yes, sir," Christian said.

"Why have you turned aside so quickly?" Evangelist pressed. Christian explained about meeting Mr. Worldly Wiseman, who persuaded him to seek Mr. Legality's help in Morality to rid him of his burden.

Evangelist asked for a description of the man who misled him. Christian described him as a gentleman who persuaded him to leave the Narrow Path for an easier way.

Evangelist then denounced Mr. Worldly Wiseman's advice, explaining the dangers of his counsel and the impossibility of Mr. Legality relieving Christian's burden. He warned against the deceit of Mr. Worldly Wiseman and Mr. Legality, and the hypocrisy of Mr. Civility.

Evangelist then called to the heavens for confirmation, and terrifying words and fire came from the hill, emphasizing the danger of relying on the Law for salvation. Christian was terrified, feeling doomed and regretted ever having following Mr. Worldly Wiseman's advice. He feared he could never return to the Narrow Way.

Evangelist assured Christian that his sins could be forgiven if only he believed. He began to revive but still trembled before Evangelist. Evangelist then gave him a stern warning about Mr. Worldly Wiseman's deceit and the eternal consequences of his advice.

Recommitted to the right path, Christian thanked Evangelist, who embraced and encouraged him.

Christian hurried back to the narrow path.

CHAPTER 5 — THE NARROW GATE

In due time Christian, arrived at the Narrow Gate. Above the gate, he saw the words, ***"Knock, and it shall be opened unto you."*** So he knocked several times, saying, "May I now enter here, though I have been an undeserving wretch? If so, I shall sing His everlasting praise!"

Eventually, a serious man named Goodwill came to the gate and asked who was there, where Christian came from, and what he wanted. He told him, "I am a poor, burdened sinner, coming from the City of Destruction. I am going to the Celestial City to be saved from the wrath to come. I've been told, Sir, that the way to the Celestial City is through this gate. Are you willing to let me in?"

Goodwill answered, "I am willing with all my heart," and he opened the gate for him. As Christian stepped in, Goodwill suddenly yanked him. Surprised, he asked, "Why did you do that?" Good-will explained, "Just a short distance from this gate, there's a strong castle where Beelzebub, the prince, and his minions shoot arrows at those who come to this gate, hoping to kill them before they can enter."

Christian said, "I both rejoice and tremble!" Once safely inside, the man at the gate asked who directed him here. "Evangelist directed me to come here and to knock, as I did, and that you would tell me what I must do."

"An open door is set before you, and no man can shut it," responded Goodwill.

"I feel like I'm beginning to reap the benefits of my hazardous journey," said Christian.

Goodwill then asked, "But how is it that you came alone?" Christian explained, "None of my neighbors saw their danger as I did, nor did my wife and children who called after me to come back. Also, some of my neighbors pleaded and called for me to return, but I put my fingers in my ears and started on my journey."

"Did any of them follow you to try to persuade you to turn back?" Goodwill inquired. "Yes," he replied, "My old friends, Obstinate and Pliable tried to turn me back but, when they saw they couldn't prevail, Obstinate railed at me and went back alone. Pliable came with me for a short while."

"Why didn't Pliable come all the way here with you?" Goodwill asked. He explained how Pliable had become discouraged at the Swamp of Despondency and decided not to venture any further. He got out of the swamp on the side closest to his home, leaving Christian to continue to the Celestial City alone.

Goodwill lamented Pliable's choice, questioning the little value he placed on Celestial Glory. Christian admitted that if he told the whole truth about himself, there would be no difference between him and Pliable. He confessed to being persuaded by Mr. Worldly Wiseman to take a different path.

Goodwill questioned if Christian followed Mr. Worldly Wiseman's advice. He admitted that he did as far as he dared, stopping only when he feared the mountain, on the way to Mr. Legality's house, would fall on his head.

Goodwill expressed relief that he had escaped that perilous path. Christian shared his gratitude for Evangelist, who found him and guided him back towards the Narrow Gate. He acknowledged his unworthiness and rejoiced in the favor now being shown to him.

Good-will assured Christian that no sincere pilgrim is ever refused entry, regardless of their past. He then instructed Christian about the way ahead, pointing out the narrow, straight path built by the patriarchs, prophets, Christ, and His Apostles.

Christian asked if there were any turnings or windings where a pilgrim might lose his way. Goodwill clarified that while many side paths intersect with the narrow way, they are crooked and wide. The right path, he explained, is always straight and narrow.

In my dream, Christian then inquired if Goodwill could help remove the burden on his back. He advised him to bear it until he reached the Place of Deliverance, where it would fall off by itself.

CHAPTER 6 — THE HOUSE OF THE INTERPRETER

Christian started preparing for his journey. He was told by Good-will that after traveling on from the Narrow Gate, he would reach the House of the Interpreter. Here, by knocking, he'd learn important lessons. Christian bid goodbye to Goodwill, who wished him well, and he continued on his way.

Upon reaching the Interpreter's house, Christian knocked persistently. When asked who was there, he introduced himself as a traveler sent by Goodwill for assistance. The master of the house, the Interpreter, soon arrived and inquired about Christian's needs. Christian explained his journey from the City of Destruction to the Celestial City and his need for guidance.

"Come in, come in!" invited Interpreter, "And I will show you some profitable things."

Inside, Christian saw a painting of a solemn man, representing a godly pastor, with his eyes lifted to Heaven, holding an important Book, truth on his lips, and the world behind him. Christian, curious about the painting, asked "What does this mean?" The Interpreter explained that the man in the painting is rare, capable of nurturing children and understanding complex matters, valuing spiritual over worldly things, and is destined for eternal glory. This man would guide Christian in challenging situations on his journey.

They moved to a dusty parlor, symbolizing an unsanctified heart. The dust was sin and corruption. Sweeping it caused a dust storm, choking Christian, showing the Law's inability to cleanse sin. But, when an assistant sprinkled water, symbolizing the Gospel, the room was easily cleaned, demonstrating the Gospel's power in overcoming sin.

In another room, Christian saw two children, Passion and Patience. Passion was discontent whereas Patience was calm.

Christian asked, "What is the reason for Passion's discontent? "The Interpreter explained to Christian that the saying "A bird in the hand is worth two in the bush" holds more significance for some people than all the teachings in the Scriptures about the value of the afterlife. This means that these individuals give more importance to immediate, tangible rewards they can have now, rather than the promise of greater, albeit unseen, rewards in the future.

Christian reflected and realized that Patience demonstrated greater wisdom for two reasons. Firstly, Patience chooses to wait for the best things, and secondly, he will enjoy his rewards when Passion is left with nothing but rags.

The Interpreter agreed and added another reason. The glory of the next world is eternal, unlike earthly pleasures, which are fleeting. Therefore, Passion had no reason to mock Patience for waiting, because while Passion gets to enjoy his rewards first, they are temporary. In contrast, Patience, who waits, will enjoy his rewards forever. This reflects the idea that those who focus solely on earthly pleasures may find themselves lacking in the eternal life, whereas those who focus on spiritual, eternal rewards will find lasting joy and comfort. This concept is similar to the story of the rich man and Lazarus, where in their lifetimes, the rich man enjoyed good things while Lazarus suffered, but in the afterlife, Lazarus found comfort while the rich man faced agony.

The Interpreter explained that what we can see and experience now are temporary, but the things that are unseen, the spiritual and eternal matters, last forever. The reason for this distinction is that the things we currently have and our immediate desires are closely related; they are easily accessible and immediately gratifying. On the other hand, worldly thinking and the anticipation of future, spiritual rewards are often unfamiliar and distant concepts to many. This difference highlights the challenge people face in prioritizing eternal values over immediate, worldly pleasures.

In my dream, the Interpreter guided Christian to a place where a fire was burning against a wall. Someone was desperately trying to douse the fire with water, but despite these efforts, the fire only grew hotter and higher. Puzzled, Christian asked, "What does this mean?"

The Interpreter revealed that the fire symbolized the work of grace operating in a person's heart. The individual trying to extinguish the fire represented the Devil, attempting to suppress this grace. To further explain, the Interpreter took Christian behind the wall, where they saw a Man with a jar of oil. This man was continually, yet secretly, pouring oil onto the fire.

When Christian inquired about this, the Interpreter explained that this man was Christ, who, with the oil of His grace, sustains and nurtures the work of grace that has begun in a person's heart. Despite the Devil's efforts to quench this spiritual fire, the grace of Christ ensures that it not only endures but flourishes. The fact that the Man was standing behind the wall, out of sight, illustrated that it's often difficult for believers who are facing temptation to recognize how this work of grace is continuously upheld in their souls.

The Interpreter then led Christian to a beautiful and pleasant place where a stately palace stood. Christian was delighted by the sight of the palace and the people walking on top of it, all dressed in gold. Curious, Christian asked if they could enter the palace.

Approaching the entrance, they observed a large group of men hesitant to enter, seemingly intimidated. Near the door, a man sat with a book and pen, ready to record the names of those who dared to enter. Guards in armor were stationed at the doorway to prevent unauthorized entry, which only added to Christian's bewilderment.

Amidst the hesitant crowd, Christian noticed a determined man approach the one with the book, boldly asking to have his name written down. After his name was recorded, this man armed himself with a sword and helmet and charged towards the guarded door. Despite the fierce resistance from the armed guards, the man fought valiantly, overcoming the obstacles, making his way into the palace.

From within the palace, a welcoming voice proclaimed, "Come in, come in! Eternal glory you shall win!" The brave man entered and was adorned with garments like those worn by the golden-clad people Christian had seen earlier. Witnessing this, Christian smiled, understanding the significance of the scene. It symbolized the idea that entering the Kingdom of Heaven requires courage, determination, and a willingness to overcome challenges and fears. Those who persevere are rewarded with eternal glory, much like the man who fought his way into the palace.

Next, Christian saw a man in an iron cage, consumed by despair. He had once been hopeful but became negligent and sinful, losing all hope of redemption. The Interpreter emphasized the importance of hope in Jesus' mercy, even when one feels lost in despair.

Lastly, Christian witnessed a man trembling from a dream of Judgment Day. The dream depicted the end of the world, the separation of the righteous and the wicked, and the man's own fear and guilt. The Interpreter told Christian to keep these lessons in mind as they would guide him on his journey.

Christian thanked the Interpreter for the insightful and meaningful experiences, feeling enlightened and prepared to continue his journey. He left the house, pondering the lessons learned and feeling grateful for the guidance provided.

Ready to continue his journey, Christian expressed his desire to leave. However, the Interpreter insisted on showing him more before he left. He led Christian by the hand into a very dark room, where they saw a man sitting caged behind iron bars, looking extremely sad and despondent.

Curious, Christian asked what this scene meant. The Interpreter suggested Christian should ask the man directly. Christian approached the caged man and inquired about his identity. The man explained that he was now what he once was not. Pressed further, he revealed that he was once a successful professor, confident and respected, and believed he was on his way to the Celestial City.

Christian, seeking to understand the plight of the man in the iron cage, asked him how he ended up in such a dire state. The man explained that his misery was self-inflicted. He had ceased to be vigilant and serious in his faith and allowed his worldly desires to take control. He knowingly acted against the teachings and goodness of God's Word, essentially inviting temptation and evil into his life. His actions angered God, and as a result, felt abandoned by Him. His heart had become so hardened by his own choices and actions that he believed he was incapable of repentance, trapped in a state of despair and hopelessness.

Christian turned to the Interpreter, questioning if there was any hope for such a man. The Interpreter asked the man in the cage if he believed there was no hope. The man responded in despair, believing he had no hope left at all. The Interpreter, however, countered, asking why he should think there was no hope when Jesus is full of mercy. The man felt he had repeatedly scorned and rejected Christ's sacrifice and grace, effectively barring himself from God's promises, leaving only the fear of judgment and wrath.

The man explained that his dreadful condition resulted from pursuing worldly pleasures and gains, which now tormented him like a burning worm. The Interpreter asked if he could now repent and turn back to God, but the man believed that God had denied him repentance and left him in his despair. The man was wrong!

The Interpreter then turned to Christian, instructing him to remember this man's misery as a lasting warning. Christian acknowledged the fearful nature of the man's plight and prayed for God's help to avoid a similar fate. He then asked the Interpreter if it was time for him to resume his journey.

Before Christian could continue his journey, the Interpreter insisted on showing him one last scene. He led Christian into a room where a man was getting out of bed, trembling and shaking as he dressed. Christian, puzzled, asked why the man was so frightened.

The Interpreter encouraged the trembling man to share his experience with Christian. The man began to recount a dream he had the previous night. In his dream, the skies turned dark, thunder roared, and lightning struck, filling him with terror. He saw clouds driven by strong winds, heard a trumpet blast, and saw a figure seated on a cloud, surrounded by thousands of fiery angels. He witnessed the heavens ablaze and heard a commanding voice call the dead to judgment. As the graves opened and the dead emerged, some rejoiced while others sought to hide.

The Man on the cloud, who appeared as a judge, commanded the angels to separate the good from the evil. The evil were cast into a fiery pit that opened where the man stood, spewing smoke and flames. The good were gathered into the clouds. The man in the dream was left behind, his sins weighing heavily on him, as he stood under the disapproving gaze of the Judge.

Christian asked what part of his dream scared the man the most. The trembling man replied, "I thought that the day of judgment had come—and that I was not ready for it! But what frighted me the most, was that the angels gathered up several people near me—and left me behind! Then the pit of Hell opened its mouth just where I stood! My conscience plagued me! And, as I stood there—the Judge continually kept His eye fixed upon me, with a look of angry disapproval on His face."

The Interpreter then turned to Christian and asked if he had taken all this to heart. Christian replied that he had, and it filled him with both hope and fear. The Interpreter advised him to keep these things in mind as they would motivate him on his journey.

Christian then prepared to leave, and the Interpreter blessed him, wishing that the Comforter be always with him to guide him to the Celestial City. As Christian resumed his journey, he reflected on the various scenes he had witnessed, grateful to the Interpreter for the valuable lessons and determined to keep them in mind.

CHAPTER 7 — THE CROSS

In my dream, I saw that the path Christian was to follow was bordered on both sides by a wall, and this wall was named SALVATION. Christian, still weighed down by his heavy load, began to run along this path. Despite the struggle caused by his burden, he continued until he reached a hill upon which stood a Cross, and just a little lower down was a tomb cut into the rock.

As Christian approached the Cross, something remarkable happened — the burden he carried on his back and shoulders simply fell off, tumbling down the hill and rolled into the mouth of the tomb, disappearing from sight.

Christian was thankful, relieved, and joyful. He felt so light, as if he was walking on air! He shouted with a joy in his heart, "Jesus has given me rest by *His* sorrow, and life by *His* death!"

Christian stood in awe, marveling at the fact that the mere sight of the Cross had eased him of his heavy burden. He was so moved by God's grace that he began to weep. Tears flowed freely down his cheeks.

As he stood there, weeping and contemplating, three Shining Ones approached him and greeted him with words of peace. The first one assured him that his sins were forgiven. The second one removed his tattered rags and dressed him in new, fine clothing. The third Shining One placed a mark on Christian's forehead and handed him a scroll with a seal on it. He instructed Christian to read the scroll as he journeyed along and to present it when he arrived at the Celestial Gate. After giving him these gifts and instructions, the Shining Ones disappeared, leaving Christian to continue his journey, now unburdened and renewed.

Overwhelmed with joy and relief, Christian leaped into the air three times. As he continued on his journey, he sang with a light heart, expressing gratitude for his newfound freedom:

"Thus far did I come, laden with sin;

Nothing could ease the grief that I was in.

Until I came here—What a place is this!

This must be the beginning of my bliss!

For here, the burden fell from off my back,

And here, the chains that bound it to me, did crack!

Blessed Cross! Blessed tomb! Blessed rather be,

The Man who there, was put to shame for me!"

CHAPTER 8—SIMPLE, SLOTH AND PRESUMPTION

In my dream, I saw Christian continue his journey until he came across a valley. There, slightly off the path, he saw three men fast asleep, shackled by fetters on their legs. Their names were Simple, Sloth, and Presumption.

Observing their deep slumber, Christian approached them, hoping to rouse them from their sleep. He called out to them, warning of the dangers they were in, likening their situation to sleeping atop a sailing mast with the perilous Dead Sea beneath them. He offered to help them remove their chains, urging them to wake up to avoid the danger.

Christian warned them, "If the one who prowls about like a roaring lion comes by—you will most certainly be eaten alive!" They then looked at him incredulously.

Simple replied, "I see no danger!"

The other two responded differently to Christian's warning. Sloth, prioritizing comfort and laziness, expressed a desire for just a bit more sleep. Presumption, showing overconfidence, believed they didn't need any help, implying that they could manage quite well on their own, thank you very much. Consequently, they all chose to continue sleeping, ignoring Christian's offer of assistance.

Christian, troubled by their decision, moved on. He was deeply concerned that these men, despite being in such a perilous situation, paid little heed to the kindness and help he offered.

Their indifference to the danger they were in and their refusal of his help to free them from their fetters weighed heavily on Christian as he proceeded on his journey.

CHAPTER 9 — FORMALIST AND HYPOCRISY

As Christian continued his journey, troubled by his encounter with the three sleeping men, he noticed two others tumbling over the wall on the left side of the Narrow Path . These two men, named Formalist and Hypocrisy, quickly caught up to Christian and struck up a conversation with him.

Christian asked, "Gentlemen, where have you come from and where are you going?" They replied that they were from the land of Vainglory and were on their way to the Celestial City in hopes of receiving a reward.

Curious, Christian inquired, "Why didn't you not come in by the gate at the beginning of the path? Don't you know that it is written that *'the one who does not enter by the gate, but climbs in some other way — that person is a thief and a robber?'*" Formalist and Hypocrisy explained that in their country, it was customary to  take a shortcut by climbing over the wall, as the journey to the gate seemed much too strenuous.

Christian questioned whether their actions might be seen as a violation of the will of the Lord of the City they aimed to reach. Formalist and Hypocrisy brushed off his concerns, claiming they had a longstanding tradition for their actions, even ready to produce witnesses if needed.

Christian pressed them, asking if their tradition would hold up in a legal trial. They confidently replied that their centuries-old tradition would be accepted by any impartial judge. They argued that being on the path to the Celestial City, regardless of how they got there, placed them in the same condition as Christian.

Christian, however, pointed out a crucial difference. He followed the rules set by his Master, while they relied on their own imaginations. He warned them that they were considered thieves by the Lord of the Path and would not be recognized as true pilgrims at their journey's end. They had chosen their own way without divine guidance and would face the consequences alone. Formalist and Hypocrisy advised Christian to mind his own business.

In my dream, I observed that Christian and the two men, Formalist and Hypocrisy, continued on their journey with little further interaction. The men asserted to Christian that they were as observant of laws and ordinances as he was, implying there was no difference between them. They speculated that Christian's coat, which they assumed was given to him by others to cover his shame, was the only distinguishing feature.

Christian responded by clarifying the true nature and origin of his coat. He explained that it was not his adherence to laws and ordinances that ensured salvation, but rather the correct entry through the Narrow Gate, which they had bypassed. The coat he wore was a gift from the Lord of the Celestial City, given to cover his previous state of moral nakedness. This coat was a symbol of the Lord's mercy and grace, a transformation from his old, sinful life symbolized by his old rags.

Furthermore, Christian pointed out the mark on his forehead, placed there when his burden of sin was lifted. This mark was unseen by Formalist and Hypocrisy, signifying an intimate blessing from his Lord. He also mentioned the sealed scroll given to him for comfort and guidance, which he was to present at the Celestial Gate as proof of his pilgrimage.

Formalist and Hypocrisy, unable to refute Christian's explanation, simply laughed and exchanged glances, dismissing his words.

Christian continued on his way, leaving the two men behind. He often reflected on his journey, experiencing moments of both contemplation and contentment. He frequently read the scroll given by the Shining Ones, finding comfort and encouragement in its words as he moved closer to the Celestial City.

CHAPTER 10 — THE HILL DIFFICULTY

Formalist and Hypocrisy caught up with Christian. They all continued their journey until they reached the base of the hill, Difficulty. At the bottom, there was a spring, and nearby, two other paths diverged from the main trail leading directly from the Narrow Gate. One path veered to the left and the other to the right, but the Narrow Path continued straight up the steep hill. Christian approached the spring, drank from it to refresh himself, and then began his ascent. As he climbed, he expressed his determination, saying,

"The hill, though high, I choose to ascend,

The difficulty will not me offend;

For I perceive the way to life lies here.

Come, take heart, let's neither faint nor fear;

Better, though difficult, the right way to go,

Than wrong, though easy — where the end is woe."

When Formalist and Hypocrisy arrived at the foot of the hill they saw how steep and high it was, and noticing the two easier alternative paths, they speculated that these less challenging routes might reconnect with the difficult path Christian had chosen, on the other side of the hill. Therefore, they decided to take these easier paths instead.

The two paths were named Danger and Destruction. One person chose Danger, which led to a vast, confusing forest. The other chose Destruction, ending up in a field full of dark pits, where he stumbled, fell, and couldn't get up again.

Meanwhile, Christian was climbing the steep hill. Initially running, then the steep incline forced him to walk and finally crawl. Halfway up, there was a cozy vine covered arbor, a resting spot for tired travelers, made by the hill's Creator. Reaching the arbor, Christian sat to rest. He took out the scroll and read it, so that it might bring him encouragement. He also examined the garment given to him at the Cross.

After some time resting, his eyes got heavy and he fell asleep, sleeping so deeply that it almost turned to night. During his sleep, he dropped his scroll.

Suddenly, someone woke him up, saying, *"Pay attention to the ant, you sluggard — consider its ways, and be wise!"*

Startled, Christian quickly got up and rushed to the top of the hill.

CHAPTER 11 — FEARFUL AND MISTRUST

When Christian reached the top of the hill, he encountered two men running towards him. One was named Fearful and the other Mistrust. Christian asked them why they were running in the opposite direction. Fearful explained that they were originally heading to the Celestial City but the further they went the more dangers they encountered. This scared them, so they decided to turn back.

Mistrust added that they had seen lions on the path ahead and were unsure if the lions were asleep or awake. The fear of possibly being attacked and torn apart by the lions terrified them.

Christian became fearful upon hearing this but wondered where he could go to be safe. He reasoned that returning to his own country, which was doomed to be destroyed by fire and brimstone, would mean certain death. He believed that his only chance of safety was to reach the Celestial City. He decided that going back meant death but moving forward, despite the fear of death, offered the hope of everlasting life. Thus, he resolved to continue forward.

Meanwhile, Mistrust and Fearful hurriedly ran down the hill, falling over themselves, while Christian continued forward on the challenging path.

Reflecting on the words of the men he had met, Christian felt a need for comfort and again reached to for his scroll. However, he couldn't find it. This realization plunged Christian into deep distress, as the scroll was his pass into the Celestial City.

Overwhelmed with fear and confusion, Christian eventually remembered that he had slept at the arbor on the side of the steep hill. Kneeling down, he prayed for forgiveness for his careless act of falling asleep and set off to search for his lost scroll. Christian's journey back was filled with sorrow. He alternated between sighing, weeping, and scolding himself for his foolishness in sleeping at the arbor, which was meant only for brief respite for weary travelers.

As he retraced his steps, Christian looked carefully on both sides of the path, hoping to find the scroll that had been his source of comfort so many times during his journey. His anxiety grew as he approached the arbor where he had rested and slept. Seeing the arbor again only intensified his sorrow, reminding him of his mistake in sleeping during such a crucial time.

As Christian drew closer to the arbor, he lamented the wasted steps he had taken, comparing his situation to that of Israel, who, because of their sin, were sent back by way of the Red Sea. He realized that he had to retrace his steps in sorrow, which he could have taken with delight if he hadn't fallen asleep. He thought about how much further he could have been on his journey if he hadn't had to walk the same path *three* times, instead of only once. Now, with daylight fading, he faced the prospect of traveling in the dark.

Reaching the arbor, he looked around in sorrow. He spotted his scroll under the bench! Overwhelmed with relief, he quickly grabbed it and placed inside his shirt. The scroll was his assurance of salvation and his ticket to the Celestial City, so its recovery filled him with indescribable joy. Thankful to God for helping him find it, he resumed his journey with a mix of joy and tears, now extra cautious as he ascended the rest of the hill.

However, before he could reach the top, the sun had set and was now forced to travel in the dark, scared by the frightening sounds of the night creatures. Remembering the warning from Mistrust and Fearful about the lions, Christian, himself, grew fearful. He worried about encountering these beasts in the dark, doubting his ability to defend himself or escape being torn apart.

Even so, Christian pressed on. As he lamented his difficult situation, he looked up and saw a grand palace directly ahead. The palace was named Beautiful, offering a glimmer of hope in his challenging journey.

CHAPTER 12 — THE PALACE BEAUTIFUL

In my dream, Christian hurried towards the palace, hoping to find lodging there. As he walked, he entered a narrow passage near the porter's lodge. Focused on his path, he suddenly saw two lions ahead and remembered the dangers that Mistrust and Fearful had fled from. Frightened, he considered turning back, fearing that a gory death lay before him.

However, the palace's porter, named Watchful, noticed Christian hesitating, and called out to him. Watchful assured Christian not to fear the lions as they were chained and placed there to test pilgrims' faith and expose those lacking it. He advised Christian to stay on the path, and no harm would come to him.

Christian cautiously continued, hearing the lions roar, but they could not reach him nor harm him.

He joyfully clapped his hands and approached the gate where Watchful stood. Christian asked if he could stay there for the night. Watchful replied that the palace, built by the Lord of the Hill, was for pilgrims' relief and security. Watchful inquired about Christian's origin and destination. Christian shared that he came from the City of Destruction and was headed to the Celestial City.

Watchful questioned why Christian arrived so late. Christian explained his delay: he had slept at the arbor on the hillside, lost his scroll, and had to retrieve it, causing him to arrive late. Watchful then decided to call for Discretion, a maid of the palace, to decide if Christian should be welcomed.

Discretion arrived and, after hearing Christian's story, called for Prudence, Virtue, and Charity. After further conversation, the four of them welcomed Christian into the palace. The whole household greeted him warmly, celebrating his arrival as a blessed pilgrim.

Inside, Christian was offered refreshments and engaged in conversations about his pilgrimage. Virtue asked about his journey, prompting Christian to recount his experiences, including his visit to the Interpreter's house, and witnessing significant events like the Man hanging on a cross, which led to the removal of his burden.

Prudence inquired about Christian's thoughts on his former country and struggles with old habits. Christian expressed his desire for a heavenly country and was aware of the challenges he still faced. Charity asked about his family, and Christian tearfully shared that his family was averse to joining him on his pilgrimage.

That night, they discussed the Lord of the Hill, his acts of sacrifice and love, and how he welcomed pilgrims. Christian was escorted to a room called Peace, where he slept and awoke singing in joyful gratitude.

The next day, Christian was shown the palace's rarities, including records of the Lord's lineage and the armory with various armors and weapons used by famous biblical figures.

Christian prepared to resume his journey, but the hosts persuaded him to stay another day to see the Delectable Mountains. The next morning, they showed him the beautiful landscape of Immanuel's Land from the palace's top, visible even to the Celestial City's gate.

Before leaving, Christian was given a full set of armor for protection. He learned from Watchful that another pilgrim, Faithful, had passed by. Christian recognized Faithful as his townsman and asked about his progress.

As Christian set off, Discretion, Virtue, Charity, and Prudence accompanied him down the hill, discussing the journey's challenges and precautions. At the hill's bottom, they provided Christian with some bread, raisins, and wine.

They prayed a blessing over him, and Christian continued on his way.

CHAPTER 13 — THE BATTLE WITH APOLLYON

In the Valley of Humiliation, Christian faced a daunting challenge. He hadn't gone far when he encountered a dreadful fiend named Apollyon coming towards him. Christian was initially scared and considered retreating but realized he had no protection for his back. If he turned around, it would give Apollyon the opportunity to shoot him. He decided it would be best to face Apollyon head on.

When Apollyon approached, he was a terrifying sight with scales like a fish, dragon-like wings, bear-like feet, and a mouth like a lion.

Apollyon confronted Christian and asked him where he came from and where he was going. Christian replied that he had left the City of Desolation, a place full of evil, and he was heading to the Celestial City.

Apollyon recognized Christian as one of his former subjects, as he claimed to be the prince of the City of Destruction. He questioned why Christian had deserted him and warned he would strike him down if he didn't return.

Christian admitted he was born in Apollyon's domain, but he found his service too harsh and the rewards deadly, referring to the saying that *the wages of sin is death*. Apollyon tried to lure Christian back, promising the best rewards his land could offer. However, Christian refused, saying he had committed himself to the King of Princes and couldn't fairly return to Apollyon.

Apollyon accused Christian of worsening his situation and told him that many who pledged themselves to his new King eventually returned to Apollyon. Christian was adamant, saying he couldn't betray his King and risk his execution as a traitor. Apollyon pointed out that Christian had previously pledged allegiance to him but was willing to overlook that if Christian returned.

Christian dismissed his previous promise to Apollyon as youthful foolishness and expressed his preference for his current King's service, wages, and country. Apollyon warned Christian of the dangers ahead and claimed that his King never rescued anyone from Apollyon's grasp. Christian argued that the apparent lack of rescue was a test of love and loyalty, and he looked forward to a glorious end.

Apollyon questioned Christian's faithfulness, citing his initial discouragement, attempts to rid himself of his burden in wrong ways, losing his scroll, and almost retreating at the sight of lions. Christian acknowledged these faults but emphasized his King's mercy and forgiveness.

Enraged, Apollyon declared his hatred for Christian's King and his intention to destroy Christian. Christian warned Apollyon to be careful, as he was on the King's Holy Path.

Apollyon straddled the whole road, and said, "I am not afraid. Prepare to die! I swear by my infernal den, that you shall go no further. Here I will spill your blood!"

A fierce battle ensued. Apollyon threw a flaming dart at Christian, who defended himself with his shield. Despite being wounded, Christian fought bravely but Apollyon was very strong. The fight was intense and lasted more than half a day. Christian grew weaker from his wounds, and Apollyon nearly overpowered him.

As the battle reached a critical point, Apollyon was about to strike a potentially fatal blow on Christian. But as God would have it, Christian reached for his sword. He confidently told Apollyon not to celebrate too soon, declaring that even though he had been knocked down, he would rise again. With a swift and powerful move, Christian struck Apollyon with a deadly thrust, causing the fiend to recoil as if mortally wounded.

Seizing the moment, Christian attacked vigorously, proclaiming triumphantly that *through the One who loved him, he was more than a conqueror*. Overcome by this unexpected counterattack, Apollyon, with his dragon-like wings, hastily retreated and flew away, disappearing from Christian's sight for a time.

Christian was left in pain and exhaustion, expressing gratitude to the One who helped him defeat Apollyon. A *hand* provided him with leaves from the Tree of Life—healing his wounds. Refreshed with bread and wine from the Palace Beautiful, Christian continued his journey, sword in hand, cautious of any further attacks. He encountered no more challenges from Apollyon in the valley.

CHAPTER 14 — THE VALLEY OF THE SHADOW OF DEATH

After passing through the *Valley of Humiliation*, Christian encountered the *Valley of the Shadow of Death*, an essential but treacherous path to the Celestial City. The prophet Jeremiah had described it as a desolate wilderness full of dangers, it was a place where no one but a Christian dared to travel.

Christian faced a challenge even more daunting than his encounter with Apollyon. The difficulties he was about to experience were to be at a whole new level.

As Christian approached the valley, he met two men running in the opposite direction, warning him to turn back if he valued his life. They had ventured partway into the valley but retreated upon realizing the peril.

When Christian asked about their experiences, they described the valley as pitch-dark, filled with terrifying creatures like hobgoblins, satyrs, and dragons, and filled with cries of misery and despair.

The men explained that they had been traveling the same path as Christian but had retreated in fear. They had nearly reached a Point of No Return and be if they had gone any further feared they would have never been able to leave.

Despite their warnings, Christian was as determined as ever. He continued his journey, with his sword drawn, cautious of potential attacks. The valley presented significant hazards with a deep ditch on one side, notorious throughout history as the place where the blind had led the blind into it, resulting in both parties perishing miserably. On the other side was a dangerous quagmire, so perilous that even a righteous person could find no solid footing if they fell into it. This quagmire was the same one King David had once fallen into. He would have been completely sucked into it had it not been for Divine Intervention rescuing him.

The path was so narrow that Christian struggled to avoid falling into the ditch or the quagmire. The darkness made it almost impossible for him to see where he was placing his feet, only adding to his challenges. Midway through the valley, he encountered the Mouth of Hell, with flames and smoke blocking his path. Unable to combat these with his sword, Christian resorted to prayer for deliverance.

Hearing blood-curdling sounds and feeling threatened, he considered turning back but still chose to continue, believing he must be halfway through. Invoking the strength of the Lord, he managed to deter the approaching fiends.

In his disoriented state, Christian mistook the blasphemous suggestions whispered by a Wicked One for his own thoughts, causing him great anguish. Eventually, he made out a voice ahead of him saying, *"Though I walk through the valley of the shadow of death, I will fear no evil; for You are with me."*

Upon hearing the voice ahead, Christian felt a sense of exuberance for several reasons. Firstly, he was comforted by the realization that there was someone else in the valley who also feared God. Secondly, he recognized that God was with him in this dark and dismal state, even though he couldn't see Him.

And thirdly, Christian hoped to catch up with the person ahead, looking forward to having company on this daunting journey.

Motivated by these thoughts, Christian continued forward and called out to the person in front of him. But that person didn't respond as he couldn't here and believed he was alone in the valley.

As time passed, the day began to break, bringing light to the darkness. Christian expressed his relief and hope, saying, *"He has turned the shadow of death into the morning,"* signifying the end of the night's terrors and the beginning of a new day.

Christian saw the dangers of the valley more clearly — the ditch, the quagmire, and the terrifying creatures, all of which were distant during the day. The light was a mercy, revealing the perils he had overcome and those still ahead.

From his current position in the valley, Christian still faced a path filled with countless dangers. The way was riddled with snares, traps, snags, nets, pitfalls, and various entanglements. Had it still been dark as it was during the first part of his journey through the valley, even a thousand lives would not have been enough to safely navigate through these perils.

Fortunately, at this moment, the sun began to rise. Christian felt a sense of relief and expressed his gratitude, saying, "His candle shines upon my head, and by His light I walk through darkness." Guided by this newfound light, he was able to reach the end of the valley safely.

In the dream, at the end of the Valley of the Shadow of Death, there was a horrifying sight. The ground was strewn with blood, bones, ashes, and the mangled remains of men, including pilgrims who had previously traveled this path. Near the end of the valley, there was a cave where, in ancient times, two giants named Pope and Pagan had lived. Their tyranny and power had led to the cruel deaths of many, evidenced by the gruesome remains.

Christian managed to pass by this dangerous area without encountering significant danger, which was initially puzzling. It was later understood that Pagan had long been deceased. As for Pope, he was still alive but had become decrepit due to old age and the defeats he suffered in his youth. He had become so feeble in mind and body that he could do little more than sit at the entrance of his cave, glaring at passing pilgrims and expressing his frustration, unable to harm them.

Christian continued his journey. When he saw the old man, Pope, sitting at the cave's mouth, he was unsure what to make of it. Pope spoke to Christian, saying that Christian and others like him would never improve until more of them were burned. However, Christian chose not to respond and passed by the cave without any harm coming to him.

CHAPTER 15 — CHRISTIAN MEETS WITH FAITHFUL

Christian, while journeying, reached a hill with a lookout for pilgrims to see the path ahead. Climbing to the top, he spotted Faithful ahead and called out to him, asking him to wait up so they could travel together. Faithful, however, refused to stop, explaining he was fleeing from the Avenger of Blood. This spurred Christian to run faster, eventually overtaking Faithful, but in his self-assuredness, Christian stumbled and couldn't get up until Faithful helped him. They then proceeded together, engaging in pleasant conversation about their respective pilgrimages.

Christian expressed his joy at catching up with Faithful, glad they could travel together. Faithful mentioned he had hoped for Christian's company earlier since Christian had started his journey before him. Christian inquired how long Faithful stayed in the City of Destruction after Christian had left. Faithful replied that he left when he heard rumors of the city's imminent destruction by heavenly fire. Christian was surprised to hear this, and Faithful confirmed that the city was abuzz with such talk, but he believed that many didn't truly think it would happen. Faithful mentioned how others mocked Christian's journey, calling it desperate, but he had believed in the city's imminent doom and thus escaped.

Christian asked about their neighbor Pliable, and Faithful recounted how Pliable fell into the Swamp of Despondency but denied it, now facing ridicule and hardship back home. Christian wondered why Pliable was so scorned if others despised the path he abandoned. Faithful explained that people labeled Pliable a hypocrite, not true to his religious profession, and suggested that God might have turned people against him for forsaking the right path.

Christian and Faithful then turned their conversation to their experiences along the way. Faithful escaped the Swamp of Despondency, which Christian had fallen into, but encountered Extravagant, who tempted him with fleshly pleasures. Christian praised Faithful for resisting her temptations. Faithful then detailed his encounter with Adam, the First in the Town of Deceit, who offered him all worldly delights and proposed he marry his three daughters, Lustoftheflesh, Lustoftheeyes, and Prideoflife. Faithful, realizing the deceit, refused and left, but not before Adam the First tried to pull him back.

Faithful also faced an attack from Moses, who disciplined him for leaning towards Adam the First's offers. He was saved by a figure with holes in his hands and side, whom Faithful recognized as the Lord. Christian identified the disciplinarian as Moses, known for showing no mercy to law transgressors. Faithful agreed, recalling Moses' previous warning about his secure life at home.

Christian then asked about Faithful's experiences in the Valley of Humiliation. Faithful met Discontent, who tried to dissuade him from the path, citing the disapproval of their relatives, Pride and Arrogance. Faithful rejected these arguments, valuing humility and God's wisdom over worldly acclaim. He also encountered Shame, who criticized religious life as pitiful and unmanly. Despite initial embarrassment, Faithful stood firm, valuing God's judgment over worldly opinions.

Christian commended Faithful for resisting Shame and shared his own struggles in the Valley of Humiliation and the Valley of the Shadow of Death, where he fought Apollyon and experienced darkness and danger, respectively. Faithful, however, had a more peaceful journey through these valleys, filled with sunshine and relative ease.

CHAPTER 16 — TALKATIVE

In the dream, as Faithful and Christian kept going on their trip, Faithful saw a guy named Talkative walking near them. Talkative was a tall guy who looked better from afar than close up. Faithful started talking to him, asking if he was on his way to the Heavenly Country. Talkative said yes, that was where he was going, and he was excited to join them and talk about important stuff.

Talkative was excited about talking on topics that are good for the soul. He was sad that many people prefer to chat about unimportant stuff. Faithful agreed, saying it's important to talk about things related to heaven. Talkative happily agreed, saying that these kinds of talks, especially about what's written in the Bible, are enjoyable and valuable.

Faithful acknowledged the truth in Talkative's words but stressed the importance of gaining insight from their discussions. Talkative agreed, mentioning how such talks could lead to understanding various spiritual concepts, including the vanity of earthly things, the necessity of new birth, the insufficiency of human works, and the essentials of Christian faith and practice.

Faithful was happy with the smart things Talkative was saying and told him so. Talkative then complained that it was a shame people didn't have these kinds of meaningful conversations more often, which he thought was why they didn't fully understand the concepts of faith and God's grace. Faithful pointed out that really getting to the core of these spiritual issues isn't just about trying hard or talking about them; it's a blessing that comes from God.

Talkative agreed, emphasizing that it's all about grace, not just our own efforts. He was proud of how much he knew about the Bible to back up this idea. Faithful then asked what they should talk about next. Talkative was up for talking about lots of different things, as long as they were useful conversations.

Seeing how Talkative was so eager to discuss deep topics, Faithful was quite taken with him and mentioned to Christian that Talkative seemed like he'd be a great companion on their pilgrimage. But Christian, who knew Talkative more deeply, cautioned Faithful that Talkative's smooth talking could easily mislead people who didn't really see through him. Christian explained that even though Talkative could talk a good game about spirituality, he didn't really live it out; he was all talk but no action when it came to his faith.

Faithful, curious about Talkative, asked Christian if he was familiar with the man. Christian confirmed that he did indeed know Talkative quite well, suggesting he might even understand Talkative better than Talkative understood himself. He mentioned that Talkative was from the same town as them, expressing surprise that Faithful hadn't come across him before, especially given the small size of their town.

Christian told Faithful that Talkative was Saywell's son and that he lived on Pratling Row. Even though Talkative was well-spoken, Christian found him to be quite a letdown. Faithful noted that Talkative came across as likable, but Christian warned him that this was just on the surface. He compared

Talkative to a painting that seems fine from afar but not so much when you look closer.

Faithful was taken aback, wondering if Christian was joking because he was smiling. But Christian was very serious, assuring Faithful of his honesty. He said that while Talkative could talk a good game, he didn't really hold strong religious beliefs. Christian pointed out that Talkative could mingle and chat in any group, especially becoming more talkative with drink, but his faith didn't run deep.

Faithful came to see that he had been fooled by Talkative's appearance. Christian went on to explain that there was no real sign of faith in Talkative's personal life, which was very different from the image he presented in public. He called Talkative a hypocrite, someone who acted worse than those without belief and treated his family and workers poorly.

Christian believed that Talkative's behavior had misled many and might ruin the faith of others. Faithful agreed with Christian, recognizing how crucial it is for someone's actions to match their words. Christian stressed how different it is to simply talk about faith and to actually live it out, likening it to the gap between the soul and the body, underlining that true faith is about what you do, not just what you say.

Christian pointed out that when Judgment Day comes, it's our actions, not just our beliefs, that will count. He compared Talkative's hypocrisy to the animals in the Bible that look clean on the outside but aren't really pure. Christian summed up by saying that people like Talkative, who do a lot of talking but don't follow through with actions, are just like noisy instruments that make sound but have no harmony or real substance, showing they don't have genuine faith or grace.

Feeling burdened by having Talkative around, Faithful shared with Christian that he was getting tired of him and sought advice on what to do. Christian proposed a way to confront Talkative with the truth about himself, which would likely make Talkative either leave them or, hopefully, actually start to change for the better.

Christian suggested that Faithful should get into a deep talk with Talkative about what true faith really means and see if Talkative's life really shows that kind of faith. Following this suggestion, Faithful started a serious talk with Talkative about how God's grace really changes a person's heart.

Talkative seemed keen to have this chat and began by saying that God's grace makes a person really against sin. Faithful wanted to be clear, so he cut in, saying that real grace isn't just being against sin; it's about hating it with a passion.

Talkative wasn't sure what the real difference was between just talking against sin and actually hating it. Faithful made it clear that it's a big deal: talking against sin is one thing, but truly hating it is something that happens deep inside you, and it doesn't always match up with what people say or do. He pointed out that there are folks who say they're against sin but then don't actually avoid doing wrong themselves.

When Faithful kept on with his sharp questions, Talkative got defensive and claimed Faithful was trying to catch him out with words. But Faithful didn't back down; he kept asking for more evidence of real grace in a person's life. Talkative, feeling the seriousness of the conversation, answered that really understanding the deep truths in the Bible shows true grace.

Faithful disagreed with the idea that just knowing a lot about spirituality equals having true grace. He made the point that knowledge by itself isn't worth much unless it's paired with action. He stressed that real grace is about more than just understanding—it's about actively living according to your faith.

Talkative began to feel uneasy with where their talk was headed and hinted that he wanted to stop. But Faithful didn't let up and continued to explain how God's grace really works. He said that grace changes you in a way that's clear for both you and others to see. It brings about a strong sense of guilt for your sins, genuine regret for your wrongs, and a sincere commitment to follow Christ and live by his lessons.

Faithful went on to say that when grace really changes a person, it touches every part of their life, including how they treat others. This change is all about a deep-down dedication to what Jesus taught. But he also admitted that it can be hard to be sure of this change in ourselves because sin and our own logic can get in the way.

Their chat with Talkative turned into a real test of whether his faith was just for show or truly deep and real. Tired of Talkative's shallow talk, Faithful asked Christian for advice on what to do. Christian's idea was to have a serious talk with Talkative about what faith really means and to ask him how God's grace was really showing up in his own life.

Talkative couldn't handle this kind of deep self-examination and backed out of the chat. Faithful, who could see that Talkative's faith wasn't as deep as he claimed, called him out on not living up to what he was saying. He told Talkative straight up that he was negatively affecting others and not living a life that matched up with what he said he believed.

Talkative, feeling criticized and not really understood, decided to walk away. This kind of exit is what often happens when someone's shallow beliefs are really put to the test. Christian backed up what Faithful did, pointing out how crucial it is to tell the difference between those who truly believe and those who don't. He talked about how fake believers can give people the wrong idea about religion and how being honest in your faith is key.

Then, Evangelist caught up with them, praising them for not giving up and pushing them to keep going on their path. He told them about tough times ahead and stressed the need for them to stay strong in their beliefs. His words and support boosted their mission and the challenges they were going to meet, underscoring the need for solid faith to get through tough spots.

CHAPTER 17 — VANITY FAIR

Then in my dream, I saw that after Christian and Faithful had passed through the wilderness, they saw a town in front of them called Vanity. In that town, there's a constant fair named Vanity Fair, open all year round. It's called Vanity Fair because the town it's in is very shallow, and everything on sale there is pointless and empty, just like the old saying goes, *"Everything is meaningless!"*

This fair isn't something new; it's been around for a long time. Here's the backstory: Nearly five thousand years back, there were other pilgrims heading to the Celestial City, just like Christian and Faithful. Some bad characters—Beelzebub, Apollyon, and Legion, and their friends—realized that the pilgrims' route to the City went right through Vanity. So, they decided to set up this fair where all kinds of meaningless stuff would be sold, and they planned to keep it going all year.

At this fair, they sell everything you can think of—houses, land, jobs, titles, positions of power, recognition, lusts, pleasures of all kinds like prostitutes, spouses, children, bosses, workers, life itself, blood, physical bodies, souls, and all kinds of treasures like silver, gold, pearls, and precious stones.

This place is also full of all sorts of deception like trickery, con-games, shows, fools, fakes, crooks, and criminals of every sort. And you don't have to pay to watch any of the theft, murder, adultery, and lying!

Just like smaller fairs have different streets or sections for different goods, Vanity Fair has different areas named after countries and kingdoms where you can find the things they're known for selling. There's a part of the fair for British goods, French goods, Italian, Spanish, German, American — each selling their own variety of vanities. But, just like any fair where one type of merchandise is the most popular, the products of Rome are especially promoted here. However, the English and some others aren't too fond of those.

I should mention that the road to the Celestial City goes right through this town that hosts the enthralling fair. If someone wants to reach the Celestial City without passing through this town, they'd have to leave the  world entirely. Even the King of all kings had to travel through this town on His way to His country, and it happened to be on a fair day too! Beelzebub, the main guy in charge of the fair, tried to tempt Him to buy his worthless stuff. He even offered to make Him the fair's ruler if He would just bow down to him.

Because He was so respected, Beelzebub took Him around, showing Him all the world's kingdoms in no time at all, hoping to entice the Honored One to give in and buy some of his vanities. But He wasn't interested in any of it and left the town without spending even a penny on these frivolous things. So, this fair isn't just some passing event; it's been around for a very long time and is quite famous.

So, as I mentioned, these Pilgrims had to walk right through this fair, and that's exactly what they did. But when they entered, they caused quite a stir. The whole place was thrown into confusion, and the town buzzed with gossip for a few reasons:

Firstly, the Pilgrims' clothes were nothing like what the traders and shoppers at the fair were wearing. Everyone at the fair stopped to stare at them. Some people called them fools, others thought they were crazy, and some just figured they were quirky characters.

Secondly, their language was different too. The Pilgrims spoke the language of Canaan, but the fairgoers only knew the language of this world, making the Pilgrims seem like foreigners wherever they went in the fair.

Thirdly, the merchants were really bothered because the Pilgrims showed no interest in buying what they were selling. They didn't even want to glance at the goods. Whenever someone tried to sell them something, they'd literally plug their ears and say, *"Turn my eyes away from things that have no worth!"* and then look up to the sky, making it clear that their thoughts and interests were set on higher, heavenly things.

Watching the two men's odd behavior, someone at the fair asked them mockingly what they wanted to buy. The Pilgrims replied seriously, "We buy the truth!" This response made the people at the fair mock and despise the Pilgrims even more, some laughing at them, others insulting them, and some even telling others to hit them. Eventually, the situation got so out of hand that the fair was thrown into chaos.

The news of the commotion reached the fair's boss, who came down promptly and sent some of his trusted associates to arrest the Pilgrims who had caused such a disturbance. The Pilgrims were taken in for questioning, and the interrogators wanted to know where they were from, where they were headed, and why they were dressed so differently.

The two men explained that they were Pilgrims and strangers to this world, on their way to their True Home, the heavenly Jerusalem. They said they hadn't done anything to deserve the townspeople's or the merchants' hostility, except for when they were asked what they wanted to buy and they said they were looking to buy the truth.

The officials who were in charge of questioning the Pilgrims didn't believe their story. They thought the Pilgrims were either crazy or had just come to cause trouble at the fair. So, they beat them, covered them in dirt, and locked them in a cage to make a spectacle of them for everyone at the fair to see. The Pilgrims ended up staying in the cage for a while, enduring ridicule and spite from everyone, with the fair's boss laughing at their plight.

But the Pilgrims stayed calm and patient, not responding to the insults with more insults, but instead with blessings. They gave kind words in return for the harsh ones and showed kindness even when they were mistreated. Some of the fairgoers, who were more thoughtful and less biased, started to speak up against the unfair treatment of the Pilgrims. These fair-minded people began to criticize the examiners for their relentless abuse.

This led to the examiners angrily turning on those who defended the Pilgrims, accusing them of being traitors and suggesting that they should suffer the same fate as the Pilgrims. The defenders argued that, as far as they could tell, the Pilgrims were peaceful and sane, and hadn't intended any harm to anyone. They even pointed out that there were other traders at the fair who deserved to be in the cage or stocks more than the Pilgrims.

This back-and-forth argument escalated until the people started fighting among themselves, causing harm to one another, while the Pilgrims continued to act wisely and composedly throughout the entire ordeal.

The two Pilgrims, Christian and Faithful, were brought in front of their judges once more, this time being blamed for the chaos that had erupted in the fair. As a punishment, they were again beaten severely, chained, and paraded around the fair as a warning to others not to support them or join their cause.

Despite this harsh treatment, Christian and Faithful remained even more composed and wise. They accepted the humiliation and shame with such grace and patience that their demeanor actually started to win over some of the people at the fair to their side. This only angered their persecutors more, who were now so furious that they sought to kill the Pilgrims. They claimed that the cage and chains weren't enough for the supposed harm the Pilgrims had caused and the deception they had brought to the fair's people.

The decision was made to lock up Christian and Faithful in their cage again until a final decision on their fate could be made. They were put back in the cage and their feet in leg-irons, leaving them immobilized and on display for further ridicule and punishment.

In their cage, Christian and Faithful remembered the words of their loyal friend, Evangelist. They found encouragement in his warnings about the trials and suffering they would face. They comforted each other, believing that the one who suffers for their faith is truly blessed. Privately, they each hoped they might be the one to endure the most for their beliefs. They accepted their situation with peace, trusting in the wisdom of the One who controls all things, until their fate would change.

The time came for their trial and potential condemnation. They were brought before their accusers for judgment. The judge was named Lord Hategood. The accusation against them was essentially the same, though worded differently. It accused them of being enemies to the city's trade, causing disruptions and divisions in the town, and converting some people to their own  dangerous beliefs, in disregard of the law of the city's ruler.

Faithful answered the charges, stating, "I've only opposed what goes against the one who is higher than the highest. As for causing trouble, I did none, as I am a peaceful person. Those who joined our cause did so because they saw our truth and innocence. They simply turned from worse to better. And regarding the king you speak of, since he is Beelzebub, the enemy of our Lord, I reject him and all his followers!"

The Judge, Lord Hategood, asked Envy if he had anything more to say. Envy replied, "My lord, I could say much more, but that would take too long. If necessary, after the other gentlemen have given their testimony against Faithful, I will provide more evidence against him." Envy was then told to wait.

Next, they called Superstition and asked what he could say against Faithful on behalf of their king. Superstition said, "My lord, I don't know this man well, and I don't wish to know him further. However, from a recent conversation with him, I gathered that he is a troublemaker. He claimed that our religion is worthless and cannot please God. He said we worship in vain, remain in our sins, and will ultimately be damned."

Finally, Flatterer was sworn in to testify against Faithful. Flatterer said, "My lord and gentlemen, I have known this fellow for a long time and have heard him speak inappropriately. He has insulted our noble prince Beelzebub and spoken disrespectfully of his honorable friends, as well as other nobility in our town. He even suggested that if everyone shared his views, these noblemen would be run out of town. He did not hesitate to insult you, my lord, who now serves as his judge, using derogatory terms."

After Flatterer's testimony, the Judge addressed Faithful, calling him a renegade, heretic, and traitor. He asked if Faithful had heard the accusations against him. Faithful requested the opportunity to speak in his defense, despite the severe accusations against him. He explained that he had only said that anything contrary to the Word of God is opposed to Christianity and requested to be corrected if he was in error.

"Secondly, in response to Mr. Superstition's accusation, I simply stated that worshiping God requires divine faith, and divine faith comes from Divine revelation of God's will. Therefore, anything added to God's worship that doesn't align with Divine revelation is nothing more than empty human religion and won't lead to eternal life.

"Thirdly, regarding Mr. Flatterer's charge, I did express that the prince of this town, along with all his followers, is more suited for Hell than this town and country. May the Lord have mercy on me!"

Then, Judge Hategood addressed the jury, who had been listening and observing the proceedings. He reminded them of the town's laws.

"There was a law during the time of Pharaoh the Great, who served our prince. The law stated that to prevent those of a different religion from growing too strong, their male children should be thrown into the river.

"Another law was made during the days of Nebuchadnezzar the Great, another servant of our prince. It said that anyone who refused to worship his golden image should be cast into a fiery furnace.

"Similarly, during the days of Darius, there was a law that anyone who prayed to any god other than him should be thrown into a den of lions.

"Now, this rebel here has violated the essence of all these laws, not just in thought, which is unacceptable, but also in word and action, which is completely intolerable! Pharaoh's law was made based on an assumption to prevent potential trouble, with no actual crime yet. But here, we have a clear offense. As for Nebuchadnezzar's and Darius's laws, Faithful openly disputes our religion! For the treason he has confessed to, he deserves to die!"

The jury, consisting of individuals with names like Mr. Blindman, Mr. Nogood, Mr. Malice, Mr. Lovelust, Mr.

Liveloose, Mr. Heady, Mr. Highmind, Mr.Hostility, Mr. Liar, Mr. Cruelty, Mr. Hatelight, and Mr. Implacable, unanimously delivered their verdict against Faithful, declaring him guilty before Lord Hategood.

Mr. Blindman, the foreman of the jury, exclaimed, "This man is a heretic!"

Mr. Nogood added, "We should get rid of such a man from the Earth!"

Mr. Malice chimed in, saying, "Absolutely! I despise even the sight of him!"

Mr. Lovelust remarked, "I could never tolerate him!"

Mr. Liveloose agreed, "Neither could I! He was always criticizing my way of life!"

Mr. Heady demanded, "Hang him, hang him! He's a sorry fellow!"

Mr. Highmind declared, "My heart strongly opposes him!"

Mr. Hostility sniveled, "He's a rogue!"

Mr. Liar proclaimed, "Hanging is too good for him!"

Mr. Cruelty snapped, "Let's send him to solitary confinement!"

Mr. Hatelight concluded, "Let's give him the death sentence!"

And so they did. Faithful was promptly condemned. He was taken from the court back to his cage and was to face the most cruel death imaginable.

They brought Faithful out and subjected him to a brutal punishment in accordance with their laws. First, they whipped him, then they physically assaulted him, and they even cut his flesh with knives. Afterward, they stoned him with rocks and pierced him with swords. Finally, they burned him to ashes at the stake. This was the tragic end of Faithful.

However, I observed that behind the crowd, there was a chariot with horses waiting for Faithful. As soon as his adversaries had murdered him, he was taken into the chariot. He was immediately carried up through the clouds with the sound of trumpets, heading toward the nearest path to the Celestial Gate.

As for Christian, he received some reprieve and was sent back to prison, where he remained for a time. But the One who controls all things and has power over the rage of His enemies intervened. Christian managed to escape from them and continued on his journey. As he went, he sang:

Well, Faithful, you have faithfully professed,

Unto your Lord, with Whom you shall be blessed,

When faithless ones, with all their vain delights,

Are crying out under their Hellish plights,

Sing, Faithful, sing – and let your name survive;

For, though they killed you – you are yet alive!

In my dream, I saw that Christian did not travel alone, for there was a companion named Hopeful. Hopeful had become so by witnessing Christian and Faithful in their words, actions, and sufferings at the Fair. They entered into a brotherly covenant, and Hopeful joined Christian on his pilgrimage. Hopeful also mentioned that there were many more individuals from Vanity

Fair who would be following them. Thus, one died as a witness to the truth, while another rose from the ashes to be a companion to Christian on his journey.

CHAPTER 18 — MR. EASYLIFE

Christian and Hopeful quickly caught up to a man named Easylife who was walking ahead of them. They asked him, "Sir, where do you come from, and how far do you intend to travel on this road?" Easylife replied that he came from the town of Fairspeech and that he was headed to the Celestial City. However, he didn't reveal his name to them.

Christian was intrigued and asked, "Fairspeech! Are there truly godly people living there?" Easylife responded, "Yes, I certainly hope so."

Christian inquired further, "May I know your name, please?" Easylife replied, "I am a stranger to you, and you to me. If you are traveling this way, I would be glad to have your company. But if not, I am content to journey alone."

Christian recalled, "I have heard of the town of Fair-speech. They say it is a wealthy place." Easylife confirmed, "Indeed, it is, and I have many wealthy relatives there."

Curious, Christian asked, "Could you tell me who your relatives are, if I may be so bold to ask?" Easylife gladly shared, "Most of the town's residents are my kindred, including my Lord Turnabout, my Lord Timeserver, my Lord Fairspeech (from whose ancestors the town got its name), as well as Mr. Smoothman, Mr. Facingbothways, and Mr. Anything. The parish parson, Mr. Twotongues, is my mother's own brother. To be honest, I have risen to the status of a gentleman of good quality. My great-grandfather was just a waterman (looking in one direction while rowing in another) and I acquired most of my wealth through the same occupation."

Christian continued the conversation, asking, "Are you a married man?" Easylife proudly replied, "Yes, indeed, my wife is a virtuous woman and the daughter of another virtuous woman. She is the daughter of Lady Feigning, hailing from an honorable family. She has been raised with such refinement that she knows how to conduct herself with people of all classes, be they princes or peasants. It's true that we differ slightly in our religious views from the stricter sort, but only in two minor ways: first, we avoid needless conflict, and secondly, our religious zeal is at its peak when it brings worldly success. We enjoy parading our religion in public, especially when it brings us praise."

Christian took a moment to confer with Hopeful and expressed his suspicion, saying, "I believe this man is Mr. Easylife from the town of Fairspeech. If that's the case, we have a rather deceitful fellow in our company, one of the worst in this region." Hopeful encouraged Christian to ask Easylife directly, suggesting, "Ask him again. He shouldn't be ashamed of his own name."

Christian approached Easylife once more and asked, "Sir, your words suggest that one can serve both God and Mammon simultaneously. I believe I know who you are. Isn't your name Mr. Easylife from the town of Fairspeech?" Easylife responded, "That's not my actual name, but indeed, it's a nickname some people have given me. I must endure it as an unfair criticism, just as other good men have endured such criticism before me."

Christian pressed further, inquiring, "But have you ever done anything that would cause people to call you by this name?" Easylife denied any wrongdoing, saying, "Never, never! The worst thing I've ever done is always have the wisdom to adapt to the prevailing customs of the times, whatever they may be. I've been fortunate to prosper by doing so. If the malicious choose to label me with such reproachful names, then I consider it a blessing."

Christian responded firmly, saying, "I had indeed suspected that you were the Easylife I've heard of, and I believe this name suits you better than you're willing to admit." Easylife attempted to smooth things over, saying, "Well, if that's your opinion, I can't change it. I'm sure you'll find me a good companion if you choose to have me along."

Christian set his conditions, stating, "If you want to join us, you must be willing to go against prevailing opinions and desires, even if they contradict your own. You must embrace religion when it seems unattractive and humble, just as when it's adorned in splendor. You must stand by it when it's in chains as well as when it receives applause." Easylife protested, "You won't be my judge or dictate to me. Let me do as I see fit and allow me to accompany you."

Christian remained resolute, saying, "You won't take another step with us unless you agree to our terms." Easylife defiantly declared, "I'll never abandon my principles, as they are both harmless and profitable. If I can't go with you, then I'll do as I did before you caught up with me—travel on my own until I find someone who welcomes my company."

In Christian's dream, he and Hopeful left Mr. Easylife behind and continued ahead, keeping their distance from him. Looking back, they noticed three men following Easylife. As they approached him, he made tipped his hat, and they exchanged pleasantries. These men were named Mr. Holdtheworld, Mr.

Moneylove, and Mr. Saveall. They had all been acquainted with Mr. Easylife in their youth, having been schoolmates taught by Mr. Gripeman, a schoolmaster in Lovegain, a market town in the county of Coveting in the north. Mr. Gripeman had instructed them in the art of prospering through means such as violence, deceit, flattery, lying, or by pretending to be religious. These four gentlemen had learned well from their master and were skilled in the same art, each capable of running such a school themselves.

In their conversation, Mr. Money-love asked Mr. Easylife about the two people on the road ahead of them, referring to Christian and Hopeful, who were still visible. Mr. Easylife replied, "They are a couple of distant countrymen who, in their peculiar way, are going on a pilgrimage." Mr. Moneylove lamented, "Oh, why didn't they wait for us? We could have had their pleasant company. After all, we are all on a pilgrimage."

Easylife explained, "Indeed, we are on a pilgrimage, but the men ahead of us are so rigid in their beliefs and hold their own opinions so highly that they lightly regard the opinions of others. If a man, no matter how godly, doesn't agree with them on all matters, they will cast him out of their company."

Mr. Saveall expressed concern, saying, "That's unfortunate. We've read about those who are overly righteous, and their strictness leads them to judge and condemn everyone except themselves. Please tell me, what and how many things do you differ from them on?"

Easylife elaborated, "Well, according to their headstrong ways, they believe it's their duty to press on in their journey in all weather conditions. But I prefer to wait for more favorable winds and tides. They are willing to risk everything for God at any moment, but I'm inclined to take advantage of opportunities to secure my life and estate. They cling to their beliefs even when everyone else opposes them, but I only uphold religion as far as the times and my safety permit. They stick to their faith even when it's despised and in rags, while I only embrace religion when it walks in golden slippers, in the sunshine, and receives applause."

Mr. Holdtheworld chimed in, saying, "Exactly, Mr. Easylife! In my opinion, it's foolish for someone with the freedom to keep what they have to be so unwise as to lose it. Let's be as wise as serpents! It's best to make hay while the sun shines. You see how the bee remains still all winter and stirs itself only when it can have profit with pleasure. God sometimes sends rain and sometimes sunshine. If they are such fools as to go through the storm, let us content ourselves with traveling in fair weather."

Mr. Easylife continued the discussion, expressing his preference for a religion that allows one to enjoy God's earthly blessings. He argued that it's reasonable to believe that since God has bestowed good things in this life, one should keep them for His sake. He cited examples like Abraham and Solomon, who grew rich in religion, and quoted Job's assertion that a good man shall lay up gold as dust. However, he clarified that they should not be like the men ahead of them, as described by Christian.

Mr. Saveall agreed, saying, "I think that we are all agreed on this matter, and therefore, we need no more discussion about it."

Mr. Moneylove added, "Indeed, we need no more discussion about this matter. For the one who believes neither Scripture nor reason, and you see that we have both on our side, neither knows his own liberty nor seeks his own safety."

Then, Mr. Easylife posed a question to his companions, suggesting a scenario where a man, whether a minister or tradesman, has an opportunity to obtain earthly riches but must appear extraordinarily zealous in some points of religion that he previously had no interest in. He asked if such a person could use religion to attain his goal and still be considered righteous and honest.

Mr. Moneylove, in response, began to address the question. He first considered the scenario of a minister seeking a higher income through increased enthusiasm and alterations in principles. He argued that this desire for a larger income is lawful as it is presented by Providence. Therefore, striving to obtain it without raising questions of conscience is acceptable.

Mr. Moneylove continued to provide his perspective on the scenario presented by Mr. Easylife. He argued that there are several reasons why it is acceptable for a minister to seek a more lucrative income by increasing his zeal and altering some of his principles:

1. IMPROVEMENT: The desire for a larger income motivates the minister to become more studious, a more zealous preacher, and overall, a better man. This improvement aligns with the will of God.

2. SELF-DENIAL: Complying with the disposition of his people by adapting some principles demonstrates self-denial, a positive trait.

3. Sweet demeanor: Such a minister tends to have a sweet and winning demeanor, making him more fit for the ministerial office.

4. Opportunities to do good: By expanding his opportunities to do good, the minister should be seen as a worthy minister rather than a covetous person.

Regarding the second part of the question concerning a tradesman, Mr. Moneylove argued that if becoming religious leads to increased market success, more and better customers, and the possibility of marrying a wealthy wife, there is no issue with it. He provided the following reasons:

1. Religion is a virtue: Becoming religious is virtuous, regardless of the initial motivation.

2. Legitimate gains: It is not unlawful to seek a rich wife or more customers for one's business.

3. Goodness begets goodness: By becoming religious and attracting a good wife, good customers, and good gain, a person is obtaining good things from those who are good themselves. Therefore, becoming religious for these purposes is a profitable endeavor.

Mr. Moneylove's answer to Mr. Easylife's question was well-received by everyone. They thought it was excellent and couldn't be argued against.

Christian and Hopeful, who had previously disagreed with Mr. Easylife, decided to challenge them with the same question when they caught up with them. They believed it would be less heated if Mr. Holdtheworld posed the question instead of Mr. Easylife.

So, they called out to Christian and Hopeful and waited for the four men to catch up. After a brief greeting, Mr. Holdtheworld asked Christian and Hopeful the question and invited them to answer it.

Christian began his response by saying that even someone new to religion could answer such questions. He argued that if it's wrong to follow Christ just for material gain, it's even worse to use Christ and religion as a tool for worldly success. He pointed out that only heathens, hypocrites, devils, and sorcerers held such views.

Christian then provided examples to support his argument. First, he mentioned the story of Hamor and Shechem, who wanted to marry Jacob's daughter and acquire his cattle. They were told they could only do so if they became circumcised. They agreed, not out of genuine faith but to gain Jacob's livestock and property. Christian referred to this as using religion as a cover for personal gain.

Secondly, he brought up the hypocritical Pharisees, who prayed extensively but had ulterior motives, like gaining widows' houses. God's judgment was severe upon them for their hypocrisy.

In summary, Christian emphasized that using religion for personal gain was morally wrong, and he provided biblical examples to support his argument.

Thirdly, consider Judas, who was driven by greed. He pretended to be religious, but his true intention was to gain money. In the end, he was lost and became the son of perdition, meaning he was condemned.

Fourthly, there was Simon the sorcerer who also used religion for personal gain. He wanted the power of the Holy Spirit to make a profit. Peter rightly condemned him, saying that his money couldn't buy God's gifts.

Fifthly, we should remember that someone who adopts religion for worldly gain will easily discard it for the world's sake. Just as Judas sought the world through religion and ultimately betrayed his Master and faith for money.

So, agreeing with the idea of using religion for personal gain, as you've done, is heathen, hypocritical, and diabolical. Your reward will reflect your actions.

After Christian's strong response, there was a long silence among them. Mr. Easylife and his friends started falling behind, allowing Christian and Hopeful to move ahead.

Hopeful agreed with Christian's sound answer and expressed approval. Christian then pondered on how these men, unable to stand against human judgment, would fare when facing the judgment of God. He questioned how they would respond when confronted by the flames of the devouring fire.

CHAPTER 19 — THE HILL LUCRE

Christian and Hopeful were ahead of the others when they reached a lovely meadow named Ease. They enjoyed walking through it, but it was short, so they quickly crossed it. At the end of the meadow, there was a small hill called Lucre with a silver mine. This mine was unique and, in the past, some people had gone off the path to see it. Unfortunately, they got too close to the unstable edge and many died or were seriously injured. Hence, locally, the hill was called 'Filthy Lucre'.

In my dream, I saw that nearby, there was a man named Lovetheworld who lived near the mine. He was inviting travelers to come and see it. He called out to Christian and Hopeful, tempting them to come and see the special mine, promising riches with little effort. Hopeful was interested, but Christian was cautious. He knew about the mine and how it had harmed many people, and he believed that chasing worldly wealth could be a trap and distract them from their journey.

Christian questioned Lovetheworld about the mine's danger, and Lovetheworld, who seemed a bit embarrassed, he said it wasn't dangerous unless someone was careless. But Christian decided they shouldn't stray from their path, suspecting that if Easylife, someone whom they knew, came by, he would definitely be lured to the mine because it matched his beliefs. Christian thought it likely that Easylife would end up dying there. Lovetheworld tried again to persuade them, but Christian was firm in his decision not to go.

Christian strongly told Lovetheworld, "Demas (his real name), you're leading people away from what's right. You've already been punished for going off track. Why are you trying to get us into trouble too? Besides, if we do anything wrong, our Leader will find out, and we'll end up embarrassed instead of proud."

Lovetheworld then claimed he was related to them and offered to join them if they waited for him. Christian asked if his name was really Demas, and Lovetheworld confirmed it, saying he was a descendant of Abraham. Christian recognized him and accused him of following in the footsteps of his dishonest ancestors. He told Lovetheworld that his behavior was deceitful and that he deserved to be punished just like his father was. Christian warned him that they would report his actions to their Leader.

After this exchange, Christian and Hopeful continued on their journey. Easylife and his friends, who were following them, were easily tempted by Lovetheworld and went over to him. It's unclear what happened to them — whether they fell into the pit, went mining for silver, or got overwhelmed by toxic fumes. But one thing was sure, they were never seen on the path again.

Christian then sang a song about Easylife and Lovetheworld:

> Easylife and Lovetheworld, in greed they do reside;
>
> One beckons, the other hastens, in wealth they take their pride.
>
> Together they share the spoils, in this world they stay;
>
> Bound by their earthly toils, beyond they do not stray.

Soon after, Christian and Hopeful came across an old statue near the road that looked like a woman turned into a pillar.

They were both intrigued and concerned by its unusual appearance.

So, Christian and Hopeful stood there, looking at the statue, unsure what to make of it at first. Then Hopeful noticed some writing in a strange language above the statue. Since he wasn't well educated, he asked Christian, who knew more, to see if he could figure out what it said. Christian looked at the inscription and realized it said, *"Remember Lot's wife!"*

Once he told Hopeful, they both understood that this statue was meant to represent Lot's wife, who had been turned into a pillar of salt because she looked back with longing while fleeing from Sodom. This surprising and impressive sight led them to have a deep conversation.

Christian said, "Wow, brother, this is a really important reminder for us, especially after Lovetheworld tried to tempt us to go see the Hill Lucre. If we had gone as he wanted, and as you first thought of doing, we might have ended up just like this woman, a spectacle for others to see."

Hopeful felt regretful and amazed that he didn't end up like Lot's wife, considering his sin was similar to hers. She just looked back, but he actually wanted to go and see. He was grateful for God's grace and felt ashamed for even having such thoughts.

Christian suggested that they should remember what they saw here to help them in the future. He pointed out that Lot's wife escaped one disaster in Sodom but still faced another one by turning into a pillar of salt.

Hopeful agreed, saying she serves as both a warning and an example. She warns us to avoid her mistake or face similar consequences. He also mentioned Korah (also known as Rebel), Dathan, and Abiram, and the 250 men who died because of their sins, as examples for others to be cautious.

Hopeful was really surprised about one thing—how Lovetheworld and his friends could keep looking for treasure when Lot's wife was turned into a pillar of salt just for looking back, without even stepping off her path. He found it even more astonishing because the statue of Lot's wife was right there, in plain sight of where Lovetheworld and the others were. They could easily see it if they just looked up.

Christian agreed that it was shocking and said it showed how hard their hearts had become. He compared them to people who would steal in front of a judge or rob right under a gallows. He mentioned that the people of Sodom were extremely wicked in the sight of the Lord, despite the blessings they had received—their land was like the Garden of Eden. This made their actions even more offensive to God, leading to a severe punishment as fiery as it could possibly be. Christian concluded that those who sin blatantly, even when there are clear examples to warn them, will face the harshest judgments.

Hopeful agreed with Christian, saying it was true. He felt grateful that neither of them had ended up like Lot's wife.

CHAPTER 20 — BYPASS MEADOW

I saw that they continued on their journey to a beautiful river, which King David called *"the river of God,"* and the apostle John named *"the river of the water of life."*

Their path followed right along the riverbank. Here, Christian and his friend walked with great joy. They drank from the river, which was refreshing and uplifting for their tired spirits. Along the river, on both sides, there were lush trees with all sorts of fruit that the Pilgrims really enjoyed. Plus, the leaves of these trees were beneficial for health, preventing sickness and the typical illnesses that travelers often face.

The river was bordered by meadows that stayed green throughout the year, decorated with lilies, adding to the beauty of the place. In these meadows, they felt safe to lie down and sleep. When they woke up, they picked fruit and drank river water again, and then went back to sleep. This peaceful routine went on for several days and nights.

So, when they were ready to continue — since they hadn't yet reached the end of their journey — they ate and drank again before setting off. In my dream, I saw that they hadn't gone far when their path moved away from the river, which made them sad, but they knew they couldn't stray from their planned route. The path started to get rough again and since they had been walking for a long time, their feet were sore. This made them feel disheartened by the challenging route and they wished for an easier way. Up ahead, on the left side of the road, there was a field called Bypass Meadow that they could get into through a stile. Then Christian suggested to Hopeful, "If this meadow runs along our path, let's go through it." He checked out the stile and saw there was a path on the other side of the fence that went in the same direction as theirs. "This is exactly what we need! It's an easier path—come on, Hopeful, let's go through here!" Christian said excitedly.

Hopeful responded, "But what if this shortcut ends up taking us off course?" "That's unlikely." Said Christian, "See, it runs right alongside the path."

So, Hopeful, convinced by Christian, left the main path and followed him over the stile into the meadow. They found the ground there much softer and easier to walk on. Looking ahead, they noticed a man named Vainconfidence and called out to him to ask where this path went.

"It goes to the Celestial Gate," he said.

"Look," Christian said to Hopeful, "didn't I say so? You can see we're going the right way."

They followed Vainconfidence, who walked ahead of them. However, as it became night, it got very dark, and they could no longer see him. Vainconfidence, who couldn't see where he was going, fell into a deep pit and died where he landed. This pit was a trap set by the Ruler of the Land to catch overly proud fools.

Now Christian and Hopeful heard him fall. They called out to him but got no reply—just the sound his final groans. Then Hopeful asked, "Where are we now?"

Christian didn't say anything; he was scared that he might have taken Hopeful off the correct path. Suddenly, it started to rain heavily with loud thunder and bright lightning, and the water began to rise around them.

Hopeful felt a sinking feeling and thought to himself, "We should have stayed on the original path."

Christian said, "Who would have guessed this path would lead us off track?" "I was worried about that from the start," hopeful responded, "I tried to warn you gently. I would have been fore forceful if you weren't older than me."

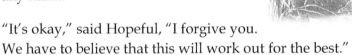

"My friend, please don't be upset. I regret bringing you this way and putting us in danger. Forgive me; I didn't mean any harm."

"It's okay," said Hopeful, "I forgive you. We have to believe that this will work out for the best."

"I'm relieved you're so forgiving. We can't stay here; let's try to find our way back.", urged Christian.

"OK but let me lead the way."

Christian replied, "No, please let me go in front. If there's any danger, I should face it first since I'm the one who led us astray."

"You shouldn't go first; you're upset right now and might get us lost again."

Then they were encouraged when they both heard a voice saying, "Focus on the road you came from; go back."

But by then, the water had risen significantly, making the way back very risky. That's when Christian had the realization that it's a lot easier to stray from the right path than to return to it.

They tried to go back, but it was so dark and the flood was so high that they nearly drowned many times. Despite their efforts, they couldn't find their way back to the stile that night. Finally, they found a bit of sheltered high ground and sat down, exhausted. They fell asleep there until morning.

CHAPTER 21 — DOUBTING CASTLE

Not far from where they were sleeping, there was a castle called Doubting Castle, owned by Giant Despair. The Pilgrims had accidentally fallen asleep on his land. Early in the morning, Giant Despair, while walking through his fields, found Christian and Hopeful asleep. He woke them up roughly and demanded to know who they were and why they were on his property.

They explained that they were Pilgrims and had lost their way. The Giant told them they were trespassing and forced them to come with him since he was much stronger than they were. The Pilgrims didn't argue much as they knew they were in the wrong.

Giant Despair then took them to his castle and locked them in a dark, dirty, and smelly dungeon. They were left there from Wednesday morning until Saturday night without any food, water, light, or help. They were in a terrible situation, far from friends and any assistance.

Christian felt particularly bad because it was his poor decision that led them into this mess. Now, Giant Despair had a wife named Timidity. When he went to bed, he told her about capturing the two prisoners and throwing them into his dungeon for trespassing. He also asked her advice on what more he should do to them.

Timidity asked her husband who the prisoners were, where they came from, and where they were headed, and he told her.

She then advised him to mercilessly beat them when he woke up the next morning.

Following her advice, he got up in the morning, grabbed a large club made from a crab-apple tree, and went down to the dungeon. There, he started yelling at them like they were dogs, even though they hadn't done anything to provoke him. He then attacked them, beating them so severely with the club that they couldn't defend themselves or escape from his grasp.

After this, he left them alone, trapped in their misery and despair. They spent the whole day in nothing but sighs and tears.

The following night, Timidity and her husband discussed the Pilgrims again, and upon learning that they were still alive, she suggested he should convince them to commit suicide. The next morning, he went to them with the same rough demeanor as before. Seeing that they were still in pain from the previous day's beating, he cruelly suggested that since they would never escape the dungeon, they should end their lives, whether by knife, hanging, or poison. He questioned why they would choose to live a life filled with so much suffering.

The Pilgrims pleaded with him to release them, but he looked at them sternly and was about to attack them again when he suddenly had one of his fits. Sometimes, in sunny weather, he would lose control of his hands temporarily. So, he had to leave them, giving them time to think about what to do next.

"Hopeful, what should we do? Our current life is unbearable. I'm not sure what's better—continuing to live this way or ending our lives. To me, death seems more appealing than enduring this torture from the Giant."

"I agree," said hopeful, "Our situation is terrible, and death seems like a relief compared to this. But remember, the Ruler of the place we're heading to has commanded, *'You shall not kill.'* We're not allowed to take our own lives, let alone follow the Giant's advice to do so. Also, let's remember that not everything is under Giant Despair's control. Others have been captured by him and have managed to escape. Maybe the God who created the world will cause the Giant to die, or he might forget to lock us up, or he could have another fit and be unable to move. If that happens, I'm determined to try my best to escape. I regret not trying earlier. But let's be patient and endure for now. We might be freed eventually, but let's not be the cause of our own deaths."

Hopeful's words calmed Christian, and they continued to bear their difficult situation together. Later that evening, the Giant came back to the dungeon to check if they had followed his advice. However, he found them still alive, though barely, due to lack of food and water and the injuries from his beating. Furious that they were still alive and hadn't taken his advice, the Giant became enraged. He told them that their situation would now be worse than if they had never been born and then left them.

At this, they were extremely scared, and Christian even fainted. When he came to, they started talking again about whether they should follow the Giant's advice to commit suicide. Christian was leaning towards the idea of ending their lives.

Hopeful then said, "Christian, think about how brave you've been until now. Apollyon couldn't defeat you, nor could everything you encountered in the Valley of the Shadow of Death. You've faced so many dangers and fears, why lose courage now?

"I'm naturally weaker than you and yet here I am in this dungeon with you. The Giant has hurt both of us, cut off our food and water, and we're both suffering here. Let's just hang on a little longer. Remember your courage at Vanity Fair, where you weren't scared of chains, cages, or even death. So, let's endure with patience."

That night, when the Giant and his wife were in bed, she asked if the prisoners had taken his advice. He told her they were tough and preferred to endure hardship rather than take their own lives. She suggested that he should take them to the castle yard the next day and show them the bones and skulls of those he had killed before, threatening that he would do the same to them within a week.

So, in the morning, the Giant took the Pilgrims to the castle yard, as his wife had suggested. "These were once Pilgrims like you," he bragged. "They trespassed on my property, and I tore them apart when I felt like it. In ten days, I'll do the same to you! Now go back to your dungeon!"

Christian and Hopeful were beaten by the Giant all the way back to their dungeon, where they spent the entire day in a miserable state. That night, Giant Despair and his wife, Timidity, discussed the prisoners again. The Giant was puzzled why neither his beatings nor his advice had driven them to end their lives.

Timidity suggested they might be hopeful of rescue or have tools to escape. Hearing this, the Giant planned to search them the next morning.

Around midnight, the Pilgrims started praying and continued until almost dawn. Suddenly, Christian realized something important. He exclaimed in a moment of clarity that he had been foolish to suffer in the dungeon when he had the means to escape. He remembered he had a key called Promise in his pocket, which he believed could unlock any lock in Doubting Castle.

Hopeful encouraged him to try it. Christian took out the key and used it to unlock the dungeon door, which opened instantly. They quickly left the dungeon and proceeded to the outer door leading to the  castle yard, which Christian also unlocked with the key.

Next, they faced the iron gate of the castle, the toughest lock yet. But the key finally opened it. As they pushed the gate open, it creaked loudly, waking Giant Despair. The Giant tried to chase them but fell into a fit and couldn't follow them.

The Pilgrims made their way back to the King's highway, finally safe from Giant Despair's reach. When they crossed back over the stile, they decided to prevent others from falling into the Giant's hands. They erected a pillar with a warning about Doubting Castle and the giant, Despair, cautioning travelers against trespassing on his grounds.

They then sang a song about their experience and the dangers of straying off the path. This warning helped many who came to that place later, as they read the warning and avoided the danger.

CHAPTER 22 – THE DELECTABLE MOUNTAINS

Christian and Hopeful continued their journey until they reached the Delectable Mountains, part of the territory of the Lord of the Hill mentioned earlier. They climbed the mountains to see the gardens, orchards, vineyards, and water fountains below. There, they swam and freely drank and ate from the vineyards.

On the mountain tops, shepherds were tending their flocks near the roadside. The weary travelers approached them, leaning on their staffs, as tired pilgrims do, they asked, "Whose beautiful mountains are these? And who owns these sheep grazing on them?"

One of the shepherds responded, "These mountains are part of Immanuel's Land, and you can see His City from here. The sheep also belong to Him because He sacrificed His life for them."

"Is this the road to the Celestial City?" Christian asked. "Yes, you're on the right path."

"How far is it to the City?" The shepherds replied, "It's quite a distance, only reachable by those who are truly meant to get there."

"Is the road safe or dangerous?"

"It's safe for those it's meant to be safe for. Good people will travel it without trouble, but wrongdoers will find it difficult."

Christian asked, "Can weary and tired pilgrims find rest here?" "The Lord of these mountains has instructed us to be hospitable to travelers, so you're welcome to refresh and rest here."

In my dream, I saw that when the shepherds realized they were pilgrims, they became curious and asked, "Where did you start your journey? How did you enter this path? How have you managed to stay on this challenging route? It's rare for those who start this journey to make it this far." The pilgrims responded as they had done before.

The shepherds were happy to hear their stories, looked at them kindly, and welcomed them, saying, "Welcome to the Delectable Mountains!"

The shepherds, named Knowledge, Experience, Watchful, and Sincere, warmly welcomed Christian and Hopeful. They took them by the arm and led them to their tents and invited them to join a meal they had prepared. They also expressed their wish for the Pilgrims to stay for a while to get to know them better and enjoy the bounties of the Delectable Mountains.

The Pilgrims agreed to stay and went to rest that night as it was quite late.

In my dream, I saw that the next morning, the Shepherds asked Christian and Hopeful to join them for a walk on the mountains. They all set out together, enjoying the beautiful scenery all around.

During the walk, the Shepherds decided to show the Pilgrims some remarkable sights. They first took them to the top of Hill Error, which had a very steep drop on the far side and asked them to look down. Christian and Hopeful saw at the bottom several men who had fallen from the top and were smashed to pieces.

Christian, puzzled, asked what this meant. The Shepherds asked if they had heard of those who made a mistake by following the teachings of Hymeneus, a heretic, and Philetus, also a heretic who did not believe in the resurrection of the saints. The Pilgrims said they had. The Shepherds then explained that the men they saw at the bottom of the mountain were those who had been led astray by these teachings. They remained unburied as a warning to others not to come too close to the edge of Hill Error.

Then, the Shepherds took them to another mountain called Caution. They asked Christian and Hopeful to look in the distance, where they saw what appeared to be several men wandering among tombstones. They realized these men were blind, as they kept stumbling over the tombstones, unable to find their way out.

Christian asked, "What does this mean?" about the blind men among the tombstones.

The Shepherds explained, "Do you remember the stile you saw a little way back from these mountains, on the left side of the path?" The Pilgrims confirmed they did.

The Shepherds continued, "That stile leads to a path that goes directly to Doubting Castle, controlled by Giant Despair. These blind men wandering among the tombs were once pilgrims like you. When they reached that stile, they chose to leave the rough main path and go into the meadow, which led them to be captured by Giant Despair and imprisoned in Doubting Castle.

"After being held in the dungeon for some time, the Giant blinded them and left them to wander among these tombs indefinitely. This fulfills the wise saying, *'Whoever strays from the path of wisdom will end up in the realm of the dead.'*" Christian and Hopeful were deeply moved and teary-eyed, but they didn't say anything to the Shepherds.

In my dream, I saw the Shepherds take them to another place with a door on the side of a hill. They opened the door and asked the Pilgrims to look inside. Peeking in, they saw it was very dark and smoky inside, heard a rumbling noise like fire, cries of tormented people, and smelled brimstone.

Christian asked, "What does this mean?"

The Shepherds explained, "This is a shortcut to Hell, a path taken by hypocrites, like those who sell their birthright like Esau, betray their master like Judas, blaspheme the Gospel like Alexander, or lie and deceive like Ananias and Sapphira."

Hopeful asked the Shepherds, "It seems like all these people were once known as pilgrims, just like us, weren't they?"

"Yes, some of them were recognized as pilgrims for quite a long time." Hopeful said, "It's sad to think that after coming so far on their pilgrimage, they ended up in such a terrible situation."

"Some didn't make it as far as these mountains, while others went beyond."

The Pilgrims then said to each other, "We really need to ask for strength from the Almighty!" The shepherds agreed, "Indeed, and you'll also need to use that strength when you have it."

At this point, the Pilgrims wanted to continue their journey. The Shepherds, Christian, and Hopeful all walked together towards the end of the range of mountains. The Shepherds then decided to show the Pilgrims the gates of the Celestial City through a special telescope from the top of a high hill called Clear.

The Pilgrims were eager to see this and went to the hilltop with them to use the telescope. But remembering the last sight the Shepherds had shown them, their hands were trembling, making it difficult to see clearly through the telescope. They thought they saw something like the gate of the City and some of its glory.

As they left, they sang:

> Through Shepherds' guidance, hidden truths unfold,
>
> Secrets from men, these guardians withhold.
>
> To Shepherds come, if mysteries you seek,
>
> In depths and shadows, their wisdom peaks.

Before they departed, one Shepherd gave them a note with directions, another warned them to be wary of the Flatterer, the third cautioned them not to sleep on the Enchanted Ground, and the fourth wished them Godspeed.

And with that, I awoke from my dream.

CHAPTER 23 — IGNORANCE

In my next dream, I saw the same two Pilgrims, Christian and Hopeful, descending the mountains and continuing along the highway towards the Celestial City. Just below the mountains, on the left side, is the country of Conceit. From there, a narrow, winding lane intersects the path the Pilgrims were on. Here, they encountered a brash young man named Ignorance, who had come from Conceit.

Christian asked him where he was from and where he was going. "I come from that country over there, a bit to the left, and I'm heading to the Celestial City."

Christian said, "You might find it difficult to get in. How do you plan to enter the city's gate?" "The same way other good people do.", replied Ignorance.

"But what will you present at the gate to be allowed entry?" Ignorance replied, "I know what my Lord expects, and I've lived a good life. I always pay what I owe. I pray, fast, pay tithes, and give to the poor. I left my country specifically to go to the Celestial City."

Christian said, "But you didn't come in through the Narrow Gate at the beginning of this path. You entered through that crooked lane. So, I'm worried that on the day of judgment, despite what you think of yourself, you'll be accused of being a thief and a robber, rather than being allowed into the city."

After hearing Ignorance's response, Christian whispered to Hopeful, expressing his concern about Ignorance's self-assurance and lack of understanding, *"There is more hope for a fool than for him!"* Christian was unsure whether to continue the conversation with Ignorance or to let him ponder on what had already been said and possibly revisit the discussion later when Ignorance might be more receptive.

Hopeful agreed, suggesting that Ignorance should be given time to reflect on the advice given, emphasizing the importance of embracing wisdom to avoid remaining ignorant. He added that it might not be beneficial to tell him everything at once and proposed that they should move on and talk with him later when he might be more open to it.

So, Christian and Hopeful continued their journey, with Ignorance trailing behind. After a while, they entered a very dark lane. There, they encountered a man bound by seven devils with strong cords, being dragged back to the door on the side of the hill they had seen earlier. Christian and Hopeful were very frightened by this sight. Christian thought the man might be Turnaway from the town of Apostasy, but they couldn't see his face clearly.

As they passed, Hopeful noticed a sign on the man's back labeling him as a "Debauched professor, and damnable apostate."

Then Christian remembered a story about a man named Littlefaith from the town of Sincere. Littlefaith, while on his pilgrimage, had fallen asleep in a dangerous passage known for many murders. Three thieves named Faintheart, Mistrust, and Guilt spotted him asleep. As Littlefaith was waking up and trying to resume his journey, the rogues threatened him. Littlefaith was too scared to fight or flee.

Hopeful asked if the thieves took all of Littlefaith's money. Christian explained that they didn't find where Littlefaith kept his jewels, so he still had those. However, the thieves did take most of his spending money. The remaining jewels and a bit of spare cash were hardly enough to get him to the end of his journey. In fact, Christian heard that Littlefaith had to beg to survive, as he refused to sell his jewels. Despite begging and doing whatever he could, Littlefaith struggled with hunger for the rest of his journey.

Hopeful expressed surprise that the thieves didn't take Littlefaith's certificate, which was needed for admittance at the Celestial Gate.

Christian agreed it was fortunate they didn't get it, though it wasn't due to any clever action on Littlefaith's part. He was too startled by the sudden attack to protect his belongings. It was more due to good Providence than Littlefaith's efforts that they didn't steal his certificate as well.

Hopeful noted that it must have been a relief that Littlefaith got to keep his jewels. Christian replied that the jewels could have been a great comfort, but Littlefaith didn't make much use of them. He was so disheartened by the loss of his money that he often forgot about his jewels. When he did remember them and started to feel comforted, his thoughts of the lost money would return and overwhelm any comfort he gained from the jewels.

Hopeful expressed sympathy for Littlefaith, noting the great grief his experience must have caused him.

Christian agreed, emphasizing the immense distress Littlefaith must have felt after being robbed and wounded in a foreign place. He mentioned that Littlefaith spent most of the remainder of his journey in sorrow, frequently recounting his ordeal to others he met along the way.

Hopeful wondered why Littlefaith didn't sell or pawn some of his jewels to sustain himself on his journey.

Christian explained that it wouldn't have been a wise decision. In the region where Littlefaith was robbed, his jewels weren't considered valuable, and he wasn't interested in the kind of help that country could offer. More importantly, if he had arrived at the gate of the Celestial City without his jewels, he would have been denied entry, which would have been a far greater loss than the theft itself.

Hopeful, trying to understand, compared Littlefaith's situation to Esau, who sold his birthright for a meal.

Christian clarified that Esau's actions were a result of prioritizing his immediate physical desires over his spiritual inheritance. He pointed out that there were key differences between Esau and Littlefaith, particularly in their attitudes towards faith and spiritual matters. Esau was driven by his immediate needs and desires, whereas Littlefaith, despite his name, valued his spiritual treasures and was not tempted to sell them, even in times of need. Unlike Esau, Littlefaith had faith, even if it was small, and it kept him from making a decision as desperate as Esau's.

Christian emphasized that people with genuine faith, even as little as that of Littlefaith, would not easily give up their spiritual treasures for temporary, worldly gains. He compared Esau's lack of faith and his surrender to physical desires with Littlefaith's perseverance in holding on to what was truly valuable, despite his hardships.

Hopeful acknowledged Christian's stern advice but admitted it almost made him angry. Christian suggested that if they focus solely on the topic of their discussion, everything would be fine between them.

Hopeful then expressed his thoughts on the three rogues who attacked Littlefaith, considering them cowards for running away at the mere sound of someone approaching. He questioned why Littlefaith lacked the courage to resist them, at least for a while.

Christian explained that while many view the rogues as cowards, few actually resist them. Regarding courage, Christian pointed out that Littlefaith had none, and even Hopeful might find it challenging to face such adversaries. Christian shared his own experience of being attacked by the same villains and how difficult it was to resist, even with his armor.

Hopeful noted that the rogues fled at the thought of Greatgrace arriving.

Christian agreed, explaining that they and their master often flee from Greatgrace, the King's Champion. However, not all the King's subjects are as strong as Greatgrace. There are varying degrees of strength and faith among them, and Littlefaith was one of the weaker ones, hence his misfortune.

Hopeful expressed his wish that it had been Greatgrace who encountered the rogues.

Christian pointed out that even Greatgrace would have struggled if the rogues got into his heart, as being physically overwhelmed limits one's abilities. He mentioned that Greatgrace himself had scars and had once despaired of life, showing even the mightiest can struggle. He recalled how these rogues troubled many strong figures, like David, Heman, Hezekiah, and even Peter, who feared a young girl due to her influence.

Christian continued, emphasizing the power of their enemy, the evil king, who is always ready to aid his minions. He described him as mighty and invincible, unaffected by conventional weapons, and laughing in the face of danger. In such a scenario, Christian pointed out, what chance do ordinary pilgrims have?

Christian advised that it's best for regular people like Hopeful and himself to avoid confrontation with such powerful enemies. He cautioned against overconfidence, as it often leads to defeat, citing Peter as an example. Peter, despite his bold claims of unwavering loyalty, was ultimately overcome by fear and denial.

Christian suggested two key strategies for pilgrims on their journey. First, to always wear their armor and carry their shield of faith, which is essential to fend off the attacks of the wicked. The lack of this shield leaves them vulnerable. Second, to seek the King's guidance and presence on their journey. He recalled how David found comfort in God's presence in dangerous situations, and Moses refused to move without God going ahead of him. With God, they can face great odds, but without Him, they will certainly fail.

Christian acknowledged his own past struggles and the mercy of God that saved him, admitting he doesn't boast of courage and would prefer to avoid further confrontations. Yet, he remained hopeful that God would deliver them from future threats, just as He had from past dangers.

Concluding his reflection, Christian sang a song about Little-faith's experience with the thieves, using it as a lesson on the importance of faith. He noted that with more faith, one could overcome great challenges, but without it, even small obstacles could prove insurmountable.

> *Poor Little-faith has been among the thieves,*
>
> *Was robbed — remember this; whosoever believes*
>
> *And gets more faith, shall then a victor be*
>
> *Over ten thousand — otherwise not even three.*

CHAPTER 24 — THE FLATTERER

Christian and Hopeful, with Ignorance following behind, arrived at a fork in the road where both paths seemed to lead straight ahead. Unsure of which one to take, they stopped to contemplate their choices. Just then, a man dressed in a light-colored robe approached and asked why they were standing there. They explained they were headed to the Celestial City but weren't sure which path to take. The man said he was going to the same place and told them to follow him.

They followed him down a path that gradually turned away from the Celestial City. Before they realized it, he led them into a trap—a net they couldn't escape from. Suddenly, the man's robe fell off, revealing his true nature, and they saw they were trapped. They lay there in panic, realizing their mistake.

Christian remembered the Shepherds had warned them about someone called the Flatterer and regretted not heeding their advice. Hopeful recalled that the Shepherds had given them a note with directions, which they had forgotten to read, leading them into this peril.

While they were stuck in the net, a person with a bright appearance and a whip came over and asked what they were doing there. They explained their situation, and he told them the man who misled them was the Flatterer, a false guide.

He freed them from the net and led them back to the correct path, asking where they had stayed the previous night. They said they were with the Shepherds on the Delectable Mountains.

He queried if they had read the note the Shepherds gave them, and they admitted they hadn't. He asked why they hadn't, and they said they forgot. When asked if the Shepherds warned them about the Flatterer, they said yes but didn't realize he would be the well-spoken man they met.

Then, the shining figure reprimanded them, *"As many as I love, I rebuke and chasten. Be zealous, therefore, and repent."* After the scolding, he told them to continue on their way and not neglect the Shepherds' other instructions.

Thankful for his help, they continued on the right path.

CHAPTER 25 — ATHEIST

Now, after some time, they noticed someone approaching them from a distance along the road. Christian said to his companion, "Look, there's a man walking with his back turned to the Celestial City, and he seems to be coming our way."

Hopeful replied, "I see him. Let's be cautious, in case he turns out to be a deceiver too."

As the man came closer, they eventually met him. His name was Atheist, and he asked them where they were headed. Christian replied, "We're on our way to the Celestial City." Atheist burst into laughter, and Christian asked, "What's so funny?" Atheist responded, "I'm laughing because you two are so ignorant. You're embarking on such a long and arduous journey, yet you'll likely gain nothing but pain from it."

Christian inquired, "Why do you think we won't be accepted there?" Atheist scoffed, "Accepted! There's no such place you're dreaming of in this world." Christian explained, "That's true, but there is such a place in the world to come."

Atheist said, "When I was in my own country, I heard about the place you're talking about. So I set out to find it and have been searching for this city for the past twenty years, but I haven't found it in all this time!" Christian responded, "We've both heard and believe that such a place exists."

Atheist said, "If I hadn't believed when I was at home, I wouldn't have traveled this far to seek it. If there truly were such a place, I would have surely found it by now because I've gone much farther than you. So, since I haven't found it, I'm going back home and will pursue the pleasures I had cast aside in the vain hope of a world to come."

Then Christian turned to Hopeful and asked, "Do you think what this man has said is true?" Hopeful warned, "Be cautious; he's one of those smooth talkers, remember how much trouble we got into last time we listened to someone like him? What! No Celestial City? Didn't we see the City's gate from the Delectable Mountains? Besides, we're supposed to walk by faith now.

Let's keep moving before that whip-wielding man catches up with us again. You should've reminded me of that lesson I'll now remind you of: 'Don't heed advice that leads you away from what you know.' I say, my brother, don't listen to him—let's hold onto our faith for the salvation of our souls!"

Christian replied, "Hopeful, I didn't ask you that question because I doubted the truth myself, but to test you and hear your heartfelt response. As for this man, I know he's blinded by the worldly god. Let's continue, knowing we believe the truth, and that no lie is of the truth."

Hopeful exclaimed, "I rejoice in the hope of God's glory!"

So, they turned away from the man, and he laughed at them as he continued on his way back home.

CHAPTER 26 — THE ENCHANTED GROUND

In my dream, I saw that they traveled on until they reached a certain country where the air seemed to naturally make travelers feel drowsy. Hopeful began to feel very sleepy and said to Christian, "I'm getting so drowsy that I can hardly keep my eyes open. Let's lie down and take a nap."

Christian replied firmly, "Absolutely not! If we fall asleep, we may never wake up again!" Hopeful argued, "But why, my brother? Sleep is refreshing, especially for tired travelers. We could use a snooze."

Christian reminded him, "Don't you remember the warning from one of the Shepherds about the Enchanted Ground? We should not sleep like others do. Instead, we must stay awake and be vigilant."

Hopeful admitted his mistake, saying, "You're right. If I were here alone, I might have fallen asleep and been in danger. What the wise man said is true: *'Two are better than one.'* Your company has been a blessing, and you shall be rewarded for your vigilance."

Christian then suggested, "To stay alert in this place, let's engage in a thoughtful conversation." Hopeful agreed, saying, "I'm all for it."

Christian began by saying, "Where should we start?" Hopeful responded, "Let's begin where God began with us. Please, go ahead."

Christian began to recite: "When saints grow sleepy, let them come together, and hear how these two Pilgrims converse. Yes, let them learn from them how to keep their drowsy eyes open. The fellowship of saints, when done right, keeps them awake, even in the face of challenges."

Then Christian asked, "How did you first think about embarking on this pilgrimage?" Hopeful clarified, "Are you asking how I first started seeking the good of my soul?" Christian nodded, saying, "Yes, that's what I mean."

Hopeful explained, "For quite a while, I was caught up in the pleasure of worldly things that were being bought and sold at our fair. I now believe that if I had continued in those pursuits, they would have led me to destruction and perdition."

Christian asked, "What were these things that you delighted in?" Hopeful replied, "I took pleasure in all the treasures and riches of the world. I also enjoyed carousing, drinking, swearing, lying, impurity, breaking the Sabbath, and more — things that lead to the destruction of the soul. But I finally realized, through hearing and considering divine teachings from you and our beloved Faithful (who was martyred for his faith and righteous living in Vanity Fair), that the end of these things is death! The wrath of God comes upon the disobedient for such actions."

Christian inquired, "Did you immediately feel convicted by this realization?" Hopeful confessed, "No, I wasn't initially willing to acknowledge the evil of sin or the damnation that follows it. Instead, when my mind was first shaken by the Word, I tried to shut my eyes to its light."

Christian asked, "What caused you to resist the initial workings of God's Spirit within you?" Hopeful explained, "Several factors played a role. First, I was ignorant that God began a sinner's conversion through convictions of sin. Secondly, I found sin very appealing to my flesh and was hesitant to give it up. Thirdly, I didn't know how to part ways with my old companions, as their presence and actions were so desirable to me. Lastly, my convictions of sin were so troubling and terrifying that I couldn't bear the thought of them in my heart."

Christian continued, "So, it appears that at times, you managed to get rid of your convictions of sin?" Hopeful admitted, "Yes, indeed. But they would resurface in my mind, and then I would be as bad, if not worse, than I was before."

Christian asked, "What would trigger these sins coming back to you?" Hopeful listed several triggers, saying, "It could be anything, like meeting a godly person in the streets, hearing someone read from the Bible, getting a headache, hearing that neighbors were sick, the tolling of the death bell for someone who had passed away, thoughts of my own mortality, or news of someone dying suddenly. But especially when I thought about facing judgment myself!"

Christian inquired further, "Could you easily shake off the guilt of sin when these convictions came upon you?" Hopeful explained, "No, not at all. They tightened their grip on my conscience. If I even contemplated returning to sin, even if my mind was turned against it, it would torment me doubly."

Christian then asked, "What did you do in response?" Hopeful replied, "I believed that I had to try to improve my life, for I thought that otherwise, I was certain to be damned."

Christian followed up, "Did you make any efforts to mend your ways?" Hopeful responded, "Yes, I did. I not only fled from my sins but also from bad company. I engaged in things like prayer, reading my Bible, weeping for my sins, speaking truth to my neighbors, and more. I did these things along with many others — too many to list."

Christian probed further, "And did you think you were in a good state then?" Hopeful admitted, "Yes, much better for a while. But eventually, my troubling convictions returned, despite all my efforts at self-improvement."

Christian inquired, "So, how did these convictions trouble you, even though you had changed?" Hopeful explained, "These sayings troubled me deeply: *'All our righteousness acts are as filthy rags,' 'By the works of the law shall no flesh be justified,'* and *'When we have done everything we should, we are yet unprofitable servants,'* among others. I began to reason with myself: If all my righteousness is worthless and no one can be justified by the deeds of the law, and even when I do all I should, I'm still an unworthy servant, then it's foolish to think I can earn Heaven by keeping the law."

He continued, "I thought this way: Suppose a man racks up a thousand-dollar debt at a shop, and from that point on, he pays for everything he purchases. But if his old debt remains unpaid in the shopkeeper's ledger, the shopkeeper will sue him and throw him in prison until he pays the full debt."

Christian asked, "So, how did you apply this to yourself?" Hopeful replied, "I thought to myself: I have accrued a great debt in God's Book due to my sins, and my reformation will not erase that debt. Therefore, even with all my current improvements, I would not be freed from the damnation my past transgressions still deserved."

Christian encouraged him, saying, "That's a sound application, please continue." Hopeful went on, "Another thing that troubled me, even after my recent reforms, is that when I closely examine the best of my actions, I still see sin mixing itself with my best deeds. So I'm compelled to conclude that, regardless of my former high opinion of myself and my actions, I have committed enough sin in my early life to condemn me to Hell, even if my past life had been flawless!"

Christian asked, "What did you do then?" Hopeful replied, "I didn't know what to do until I shared my thoughts with Faithful, as we were well-acquainted. He told me that unless I could obtain the righteousness of a Man who never sinned, neither my own righteousness nor all the righteousness in the world could save me."

Christian questioned, "Did you believe he was telling the truth?" Hopeful confessed, "If he had told me this when I was still pleased and content with my own improvements, I would have considered him a fool for his advice. But now, since I recognize my own error and the sin that clings to even my best efforts, I was compelled to embrace his perspective."

Christian further inquired, "Did you think, when he first suggested it, that such a Man could be found, of whom it could justly be said that He never committed any sin?" Hopeful admitted, "At first, his words did sound strange, but after some more conversation with him, I became fully convinced."

Christian asked, "Did you inquire from Faithful who this Man was and how you could be justified by Him?" Hopeful replied, "Yes, and he told me it was the Lord Jesus, who dwells at the right hand of the Most High God. He explained that I must be justified by Him through faith in what He Himself accomplished during His earthly life and what He suffered when He hung on the cross. I asked him further how that Man's righteousness could be effective in justifying another before God, and he told me that He *was* the mighty God, and that both His life and His death were not for Himself, but for *me*, and the worthiness of His deeds would be accredited to me if I believed in Him."

Christian asked, "So, what did you do next?" Hopeful replied, "I had objections against believing because I thought He was not willing to save me."

Christian inquired, "What did Faithful say to you then?" Hopeful explained, "He told me to go to Him and see for myself. I mentioned that it might be presumptuous, but he said, 'Not at all, for I was invited to come.' Then he gave me a book of Jesus, in His own words, to encourage me further. He said that every jot and tittle of that book stood firmer than the foundation of Heaven and earth."

Hopeful continued, "I asked Faithful what I should do when I go to Him, and he told me I must implore the Father on my knees and with all my heart and soul to reveal the Lord Jesus to me. I inquired further how to make my petition, and he said, 'Go, and you shall find Him on a mercy-seat, where He sits all year long to grant pardon and forgiveness to those who come.'"

Hopeful added, "I told him I didn't know what to say when I go. He advised me to say something like this: 'God be merciful to me, a sinner, and make me know and believe in Jesus Christ. For I see that if He had not provided His perfect righteousness, or if I do not have faith in His righteousness, then I am utterly without hope. Lord, I have heard that You are a merciful God and have ordained that Your Son, Jesus Christ, should be the Savior of the world. Moreover, You are willing to bestow Him upon such a poor sinner as me — and I am indeed a poor sinner. Lord, please magnify Your grace in the salvation of my soul through Your Son, Jesus Christ. Amen.'"

Christian asked, "And did you do as you were instructed?" Hopeful replied, "Yes, repeatedly."

Christian then inquired, "Did the Father reveal His Son to you?" Hopeful said, "Not at the first, second, third, fourth, fifth, or even the sixth time."

Christian asked, "What did you do then?" Hopeful admitted, "I didn't know what to do!"

Christian probed further, "Did you ever consider giving up praying?" Hopeful responded, "Yes, many times, twice over!"

Christian asked, "What prevented you from giving up?" Hopeful explained, "I believed what Faithful had told me was true, namely, that without the righteousness of Christ, all the world could not save me. Therefore, I thought that if I stopped praying, I would die, and I dare not die except at the throne of grace. Then this thought came to mind: *'Though it seems slow in coming, wait patiently, for it will surely take place.'* So I continued praying until the Father revealed His Son to me."

Christian inquired, "How was He revealed to you?" Hopeful described, "I did not see Him with my bodily eyes but with the eyes of my understanding. It happened this way: One day, I was very sad, perhaps sadder than at any other time in my life. This sadness arose from a fresh awareness of the enormity and vileness of my sins. I was then expecting nothing but Hell and everlasting damnation for my soul. Suddenly, I thought I saw the Lord Jesus look down from Heaven upon me and say, *'Believe on the Lord Jesus Christ, and you shall be saved.'*"

Hopeful continued, "But I replied, 'Lord, I am a dreadful sinner – a very dreadful sinner.'" He recounted, "And He answered, *'My grace is sufficient for you.'*"

Hopeful continued, "Then I said, 'But, Lord, what is believing?' And then I saw from that saying, *'He who comes to Me shall never hunger, and he who believes on Me shall never thirst,'* that believing and coming were one and the same; and that he who came, that is, he who ran out in his heart and affections after salvation by Christ, indeed believed in Christ."

He added, "Then tears welled up in my eyes, and I asked further: 'But Lord, may such a vile sinner as I am indeed be accepted by You and be saved by You?' And I heard Him say, *'Whoever comes to Me, I will never cast out.'*"

Hopeful continued, "Then I said, 'But how, Lord, in my coming to You, must I properly think of You that my faith may be rightly placed upon You?' And He said, *'Christ Jesus came into the world to save sinners.' 'He is the end of the law for righteousness to everyone who believes.' 'He died for our sins and rose again for our justification.' 'He loved us and washed us from our sins in His own blood.' 'He is the mediator between God and men.' 'He ever lives to make intercession for us.'"*

He went on, "From all of this, I gathered that I must look for righteousness in His person and for atonement for my sins by His blood. Also, that what He did in obedience to His Father's law and in submitting to its penalty was not for Himself but for the one who will accept it for his salvation and be thankful. That was me!"

Hopeful concluded, "And now my heart was full of joy, my eyes were full of tears, and my affections were running over with love to the name, ways, and people of Jesus Christ."

Christian asked, "This was a revelation of Christ to your soul indeed! But tell me particularly, what effect this encounter had on your spirit." Hopeful replied, "First, it made me see that all the world, notwithstanding all its boasted righteousness, is in a state of condemnation."

"Secondly," he continued, "it made me see that God the Father is both just and the Justifier of the one who believes in Jesus."

"Thirdly," Hopeful added, "it made me greatly ashamed of the vileness of my former life and confounded me with the sense of my own ignorance; for I never had a thought in my heart before now that so showed me the beauty of Jesus Christ."

"Lastly," he emphasized, "it made me love a holy life and long to do something for the honor and glory of the name of the Lord Jesus. Yes, I thought that had I now a thousand gallons of blood in my body, I could spill it all for the sake of the Lord Jesus."

CHAPTER 27 — IGNORANCE REJOINS THE PILGRIMS

In my dream, I saw that Hopeful noticed Ignorance, who they had left behind, was now following them. Hopeful pointed out to Christian that Ignorance was still trailing them. Christian agreed, noting that Ignorance didn't seem interested in joining them. Hopeful thought it wouldn't have been bad if Ignorance had stayed with them. Christian believed Ignorance thought differently.

Hopeful suggested they wait for him, so they did. Then Christian called out to Ignorance, inviting him to catch up and asking why he was staying so far back. Ignorance replied that he preferred walking alone unless he found better company.

Christian whispered to Hopeful that he was right about Ignorance not wanting their company. But he still called out to Ignorance, suggesting they chat to pass the time and asked how things were between him and God. Ignorance said he was hopeful because he often had comforting thoughts.

When Christian asked what these thoughts were, Ignorance said he thought about God and Heaven. Christian pointed out that even devils and damned souls think about them. Ignorance argued that he not only thought about them but also desired them. Christian countered that many desire heaven but never reach it, comparing Ignorance to a lazy person who desires but achieves nothing.

Ignorance insisted he thought about God and Heaven and had given up everything for them. Christian doubted this, saying it's hard to give up everything, and questioned how Ignorance knew he had done so. Ignorance claimed his heart told him. Christian warned that trusting one's heart can be foolish, but Ignorance insisted his heart was good. Christian questioned how he could be sure, and Ignorance said his heart gave him hope for Heaven. Christian suggested this could be deceptive, as one can feel hopeful yet be wrong. Ignorance believed his hope was valid since his heart and life were in harmony.

Christian asked Ignorance how he knew his heart and actions were in harmony. Ignorance replied that he just felt it in his heart. Christian argued that only God's word is a reliable judge in these matters, and personal feelings alone aren't enough. Ignorance wondered if good thoughts and living according to God's commandments weren't indicators of a good heart and life. Christian agreed these are good, but pointed out it's one thing to actually have a good heart and life and another to just think you do.

Ignorance asked for clarification on what good thoughts and a life aligned with God's commandments look like. Christian explained that good thoughts can be about ourselves, God, Christ, or other things, and they should match what the Bible says. For example, the Bible states that naturally, people are not righteous and always think evil thoughts. So, if someone acknowledges this about themselves, their thoughts align with the Bible.

Ignorance couldn't accept that his heart was that bad. Christian countered that this meant Ignorance never truly understood himself. He continued, saying our thoughts about ourselves and our actions are good when they match the Bible's views. The Bible says human ways are wrong and everyone has strayed from God. So, if someone realizes and humbly accepts this, their thoughts are in line with the Bible.

Regarding thoughts about God, Christian said they are good when they align with what the Bible teaches about God's nature and attributes. For example, understanding that God knows us better than we know ourselves, that He sees our sins even when we don't, and that our best efforts are still flawed in His eyes.

Ignorance wondered if Christian thought he was foolish enough to believe God couldn't see his flaws or that he could please God with his actions. Christian asked Ignorance what he believed about this. Ignorance briefly stated that he thought he needed to believe in Christ to be justified.

Christian challenged Ignorance, asking how he could believe in Christ without recognizing his own need for Him. He pointed out that Ignorance didn't see his own sins and had too high an opinion of himself, making it impossible for him to understand the need for Christ's righteousness to justify him before God. Ignorance insisted his beliefs were fine regardless.

Christian asked Ignorance to clarify his beliefs. Ignorance believed that Christ died for sinners and that he would be justified before God through his obedience to God's law, thinking Christ would make his religious duties acceptable to God.

Christian responded that Ignorance's faith was imaginary and false, as it was based on his own righteousness rather than Christ's. He argued that Ignorance believed Christ justified his actions, not his person, and was mistaken in thinking his actions would make him right with God. Christian warned that such faith was deceitful and wouldn't save him from God's judgment. True faith, he explained, recognizes one's lost condition and relies on Christ's righteousness, which fulfills the law's requirements.

Ignorance objected, fearing that relying only on Christ's righteousness would encourage sinful living. Christian rebuked him for his ignorance, explaining that he didn't understand justifying righteousness or how to protect his soul from God's wrath through Christ alone. He added that Ignorance misunderstood the true effects of faith.

Hopeful then asked Ignorance if God had revealed Christ to his heart. Ignorance dismissed this as foolishness. Hopeful explained that Christ can only be truly known when God reveals Him. Ignorance disagreed, claiming his beliefs were as valid as theirs but without their foolish notions.

Christian emphasized the seriousness of the matter, asserting that no one can know Christ without God's revelation and that true faith must be powered by God's might. He told Ignorance that he was unaware of how this faith worked in his own soul and urged him to realize his wretchedness and seek salvation through Christ's righteousness.

Ignorance told Christian and Hopeful that they were moving too fast for him and that he needed to slow down and stay behind. They warned Ignorance that ignoring good advice repeatedly would lead to trouble. They said if he didn't listen, he'd regret it and reminded him that good advice is valuable and should be taken seriously.

Christian then told Hopeful they should continue walking alone, as Ignorance was falling behind. Christian expressed pity for Ignorance, fearing his end would be unfortunate. Hopeful noted that many people in their town were like Ignorance, some even pretending to be pilgrims. He wondered how many more there must be in Ignorance's hometown. Christian quoted a scripture about people being blinded and hardened so they wouldn't understand and turn to be healed. He then asked Hopeful what he thought about people like Ignorance and whether they ever truly realized their sinful state and felt fear for their situation.

Hopeful suggested Christian should answer, given his greater experience. Christian thought such people might occasionally realize their sins, but their ignorance led them to misunderstand these realizations as harmful, so they tried to suppress them and continued in self-deception.

Hopeful agreed that fear can be beneficial at the start of one's spiritual journey. Christian confirmed this, saying that the right kind of *fear is the beginning of wisdom*. Hopeful asked what the right fear looked like. Christian explained that it arises from understanding one's sins, leads one to seek salvation in Christ, and results in a deep respect for God, His word, and His ways, keeping the soul cautious and avoiding anything that dishonors God.

Hopeful agreed with Christian's explanation and then asked if they were near the end of the Enchanted Ground. Christian asked if Hopeful was tired of their conversation, but Hopeful just wanted to know their location. Christian said they had less than two miles to go and suggested they continue their discussion. He reiterated that the ignorant don't realize that their fears and convictions are actually for their good, so they try to suppress them. Hopeful then asked how these people try to suppress their convictions.

Christian explained to Hopeful the reasons why people like Ignorance suppress their fears and convictions. First, they mistakenly think these fears are caused by the devil, not realizing they're actually from God, so they resist them. Second, they falsely believe these fears destroy their faith, which they don't really have, leading them to harden their hearts. Third, they wrongly assume they shouldn't feel fear, becoming more presumptuous and overconfident. Lastly, they resist these fears because they threaten their self-righteousness.

Hopeful related to this, recalling his own experience before he truly understood himself. Christian then suggested they move on from discussing Ignorance and focus on a more beneficial topic. Hopeful agreed and asked Christian to start the new discussion.

Christian asked if Hopeful remembered someone named Temporary from about ten years ago, who was well-known in religious circles. Hopeful knew him; he lived near a man named Turnback in a town close to Honesty. Christian noted that Temporary was once deeply aware of his sins and their consequences.

Hopeful remembered Temporary visiting him often, showing much emotion and seeming genuinely repentant. But as they both knew, not everyone who outwardly shows devotion is genuinely saved. Christian mentioned that Temporary had planned to go on a pilgrimage but changed after meeting someone named Saveself, becoming distant from Christian.

Hopeful proposed they analyze why Temporary and others like him suddenly fall away from their faith. Christian agreed this would be insightful. Hopeful outlined four reasons for backsliding: Firstly, their minds aren't truly changed, so when guilt fades, they revert to sin. This is *like a sick dog returning to its vomit*. Secondly, their initial desire for heaven is only due to fear of hell. When this fear lessens, so does their desire for salvation, leading them back to sin.

Another reason is the overpowering fear of men, which acts as a snare. While the fear of hell is present, they're interested in heaven. But when this fear subsides, they worry about earthly losses or troubles and return to worldly ways.

Hopeful added that another obstacle for these individuals is the shame associated with religion. They are proud and see religion as lowly and contemptible. So, when their fear of hell and divine wrath fades, they revert to their previous sinful ways.

Also, the feelings of guilt and thoughts of terrifying consequences are unbearable for them. They don't want to confront their misery before it actually happens, even though recognizing it might lead them to seek safety. However, they avoid even thinking about guilt and terror. Once they overcome their initial fears of God's wrath, they willingly harden their hearts and choose paths that make them even more callous.

Christian agreed, pointing out that the root of the problem is their lack of genuine change in mind and heart. They are like a criminal who appears to be repentant in front of a judge out of fear of punishment, not because of true remorse. If set free, such a person would likely continue their criminal behavior because their mindset hasn't really changed.

Hopeful asked Christian to describe how these individuals backslide. Christian outlined the process:

1. They deliberately stop thinking about God, death, and judgment.

2. Gradually, they abandon private religious practices like personal prayer, controlling their desires, and feeling sorrow for sin.

3. They avoid the company of enthusiastic and devout Christians.

4. They become indifferent to public religious activities like listening to sermons, reading scripture, and participating in godly fellowship.

5. They start to criticize and find faults in devout people as an excuse to abandon religion themselves.

6. They begin associating with immoral and worldly people.

7. They engage in immoral and indecent conversations in private, taking encouragement from the failings of those considered honest.

8. They start openly engaging in minor sins.

9. As they become more hardened, they openly reveal their true sinful nature.

Christian concluded that these people are heading towards eternal misery due to their self-deception, unless they experience a miraculous intervention of grace.

CHAPTER 28 — BEULAH LAND

In my dream, the Pilgrims had moved beyond the Enchanted Ground and entered the country of Beulah. The air in Beulah was sweet and pleasant, a place where the sun shone both day and night. It was a joyful land, filled with the singing of birds, beautiful new flowers each day, and the soothing song of the turtle dove.

This delightful country was beyond the Valley of the Shadow of Death and out of the reach of Giant Despair, so the Pilgrims couldn't even see Doubting Castle from there. They were now close to the City they had been traveling towards, and in Beulah, they often encountered the Shining Ones, as this land was on the borders of Heaven.

In Beulah, the relationship between the Bride (symbolizing the believers) and the Bridegroom (symbolizing Jesus) was renewed and celebrated. This was a place of great abundance, where their long journey's desires were finally met. They heard voices from the City proclaiming salvation and rewards.

The residents of this country referred to the Pilgrims as 'The holy people,' 'The redeemed of the Lord,' and 'Sought out ones.' The joy of the Pilgrims in this land was greater than at any other point in their journey. As they neared the City, its beauty became clearer. It was a radiant place, built of pearls and precious stones, with streets of pure gold that shone brilliantly in the sunlight. This splendor made Christian and Hopeful lovesick with longing for the City. They stayed in Beulah for a while, expressing their deep yearning for their Beloved.

As they regained strength to manage their lovesickness, they continued their journey, getting closer to the City. They passed through orchards, vineyards, and gardens with open gates along the highway. Upon inquiring, they learned that these beautiful places belonged to the King, meant for His delight and to refresh Pilgrims.

A gardener invited them to enjoy the delicacies of the vineyards and showed them the walkways and arbors where the King liked to spend time. The Pilgrims tarried in this serene and delightful place, taking the time to rest and sleep.

In my dream, I noticed that the Pilgrims were talking more in their sleep than they had at any other point during their journey. As I pondered this, the gardener explained to me that the nature of the grapes from these vineyards caused those who ate them and fell asleep to speak sweetly in their slumber.

When the Pilgrims awoke, they prepared to continue their journey towards the City. However, the City was made of pure gold and shone so brightly with the reflection of the sun that they couldn't look at it directly. They needed a special instrument to view it without being overwhelmed by its brilliance.

As they journeyed on, two men dressed in clothes that sparkled like gold and with faces that shone like light met them. These men inquired about the Pilgrims' origins, where they had stayed, the challenges and dangers they had faced, as well as the comforts and pleasures they had experienced. The Pilgrims shared their story with them.

The men then informed the Pilgrims that they only had two more challenges to overcome before reaching the City. Christian and Hopeful invited these shining men to accompany them, to which they agreed, but they emphasized that the Pilgrims must reach the City through their own faith.

In my dream, I saw them continue together until they came within sight of the gate of the City.

o

CHAPTER 29 — THE RIVER OF DEATH

In my dream, I saw that as the Pilgrims approached the gate of the City, they encountered a significant obstacle: a deep river with no bridge to cross it. This sight bewildered the Pilgrims, especially Christian, who became fearful at the prospect of crossing it. The men accompanying them explained that the only way to the gate was to go through the river, and there was no alternate route except for the one taken by Enoch and Elijah.

Christian began to ndair, searching for any way to avoid the river, but there was none. When they asked about the depth of the waters, the men told them that the depth would vary depending on their faith in the King of the City.

Upon entering the river, Christian started to sink and was overwhelmed with fear, feeling as if he was drowning under the waves. Hopeful, on the other hand, felt a firm bottom and tried to encourage Christian, assuring him of the firmness of the ground and the closeness of the gate.

Christian, however, was gripped by terror and despair, haunted by the sins of his past and fearful that he would perish in the river without reaching the promised land. He seemed to lose his sense of coherence and could only express his fear of dying in the river.

Hopeful, understanding Christian's troubled state, worked hard to keep him afloat, encouraging him by pointing out the gate and the people waiting to receive them. Christian, in his despair, felt that he was unworthy and that the people were waiting only for Hopeful. Despite Christian's struggle with his fears and doubts, Hopeful remained steadfast, continuing to offer support and reassurance.

In my dream, Christian, overwhelmed by his struggles in the river, lamented that his sins had led to his current predicament and believed that God had abandoned him. Hopeful, however, reminded Christian of a scripture that described how the righteous face no struggles at death, their strength remaining firm. He assured Christian that the difficulties and distress they were experiencing in the waters were not signs of God's abandonment but a test of their faith and a call to remember God's previous goodness and rely on Him in their current troubles.

This reassurance prompted Christian to reflect deeply. Hopeful then encouraged him further, invoking the healing power of Jesus Christ. Inspired by this, Christian suddenly regained his hope and vision, declaring that he could see Christ again, who assured him of His presence in times of trouble and promised that the waters would not overwhelm him.

Revitalized by this renewed faith, both Pilgrims found their courage, and the obstacles and hindrances from their enemy ceased. Christian then felt solid ground beneath him and realized that the rest of the river was shallow. With renewed strength and faith, they both successfully crossed the river.

CHAPTER 30 — THE CELESTIAL CITY

Upon reaching the other side of the river, Christian and Hopeful were greeted again by the two Shining Men who had been waiting for them. The Shining Men revealed themselves as ministering spirits sent to serve those who are heirs of salvation, welcoming the Pilgrims warmly.

Together, they proceeded towards the gate of the City, which was situated on a great hill. Despite the hill's steepness, the Pilgrims ascended with ease, aided by the Shining Men. Notably, Christian and Hopeful had left their mortal garments in the river; they entered the waters clothed but emerged without these earthly clothes, signifying a transformation from their worldly existence.

As they approached the City, they moved with agility and speed. The City was founded upon a foundation higher than the clouds, symbolizing its heavenly nature. Throughout their ascent, they engaged in pleasant conversations with the Shining Ones, feeling comforted and exhilarated by having successfully crossed the river and now being in the company of such glorious beings.

The Shining Ones described the splendor of the City to the Pilgrims. They spoke of its indescribable beauty and glory, referring to it as Mount Zion, the heavenly Jerusalem, home to countless angels and the spirits of just men made perfect. They told Christian and Hopeful that they were heading to God's paradise, where they would see the Tree of Life and partake in its eternal fruits. Upon their arrival, they would be given white robes and would have the privilege of walking and talking with the King every day for all eternity.

This description filled the Pilgrims with awe and anticipation as they neared the end of their long and arduous journey, about to enter a place of eternal joy and fellowship with the divine.

In my dream, as Christian and Hopeful neared the gate of the City with the Shining Ones, they were assured that in this holy place, they would never again experience the sorrows and afflictions of their earthly lives, such as pain, sickness, and death. They were told that these hardships had passed away and that they were heading towards a place of eternal peace and righteousness, where they would join biblical figures like Abraham, Isaac, Jacob, and the prophets, who had been taken away from the evils of the world.

Curious, the Pilgrims asked what they would do in the holy City. The Shining Ones explained that there, the Pilgrims would receive the rewards for all their toils and sorrows endured during their earthly pilgrimage. They would reap the fruits of their prayers, tears, and sufferings endured for the King. They would wear crowns of righteousness and constantly bask in the presence of the Holy One, seeing Him as He truly is.

Their service to God, which had been challenging due to the frailties of their earthly bodies, would now be unimpeded and filled with praise, worship, and thanksgiving. They would delight in seeing and hearing God and enjoy reunions with friends who had gone before them and welcome those who would follow.

In the City, they would be adorned with glory and majesty, accompanying the King of glory. They would be with Him when He returns triumphantly, sit with Him in judgment, and even have a voice in the judgment against their enemies. The promise was that they would be with the Lord forever.

As they approached the gate, a company of the heavenly host came out to meet them, signifying their welcome into the eternal kingdom. This moment marked the culmination of their long and arduous journey, a transition from their earthly pilgrimage to their eternal home.

In my dream, as Christian and Hopeful reached the gate of the City, the two Shining Ones proudly declared that these were the men who had loved the Lord in the world and had forsaken all for His holy name. They had been sent to escort the Pilgrims on the final leg of their journey so they could enter the City and joyfully see their Redeemer.

The heavenly hosts welcomed them with great celebration, proclaiming, *"Blessed are those who are invited to the marriage supper of the Lamb!"* This exclamation was met with the arrival of several of the King's trumpeters, dressed in radiant white. Their trumpets resounded through the heavens, filling the air with melodious and jubilant sounds.

The trumpeters greeted Christian and Hopeful with countless welcomes, forming a protective circle around them. They guided the Pilgrims through the higher realms, their music blending with joyful expressions, signaling how delighted they were to receive them.

At this point, Christian and Hopeful felt as though they were already in Heaven. The presence of angels and their harmonious voices, along with the sight of the City itself, was overwhelming. The sound of the City bells seemed to ring in welcome, and the Pilgrims were filled with immense joy at the thought of their eternal home in such divine company.

As they approached the gate, they saw inscribed in gold the words, *"Blessed are those who obey His commandments — that they may have the right to the Tree of Life, and may enter through the gates into the City."* This inscription was a testament to the journey they had undertaken, a journey of faith, obedience, and devotion, leading them to this moment of glorious culmination.

In my dream, as Christian and Hopeful stood at the gate, the Shining Men instructed them to call out. When they did, several esteemed figures, including Enoch, Moses, and Elijah, looked over the gate. These figures were informed that the Pilgrims had journeyed from the city of Destruction out of their love for the King of this place.

The Pilgrims then presented their certificates, which they had received at the beginning of their journey. These certificates were taken to the King. After reading them, the King inquired about the whereabouts of the men, and upon learning they were outside, He commanded that the gates be opened to the righteous, allowing the faithful to enter.

As Christian and Hopeful entered the gate, they underwent a magnificent transformation; they were adorned with clothing that shone like gold. They were met with harps for worship and crowns as a symbol of honor. The bells of the City rang joyously, and they were welcomed with the words, *"Enter into the joy of your Lord!"* The Pilgrims themselves sang praises with full hearts.

As I looked into the City, it gleamed like the sun, with streets paved in gold. The inhabitants wore crowns, held palm branches, and played golden harps, singing praises. Angels sang ceaselessly, *"Holy, holy, holy, is the Lord!"* After this heavenly welcome, the gates of the City were closed. Witnessing all this glory, I found myself longing to be among them.

My attention then turned to Ignorance, who approached the river. Unlike Christian and Hopeful, Ignorance crossed the river easily, helped by a ferryman named Vainhope. This contrast highlighted the different journeys of those who seek the City, some finding easy passage but perhaps not the true entrance to the eternal City, as Christian and Hopeful did through their faith and perseverance.

In my dream, Ignorance reached the hill and approached the gate alone, without any welcoming party or encouragement. When he arrived, he read the inscription above the gate and confidently knocked, expecting to be granted entry. However, when questioned by the gatekeepers about his origins and intentions, Ignorance claimed he had dined in the presence of the King and heard His teachings.

The crucial moment came when the gatekeepers asked for his certificate, which was necessary to present to the King for entry. Ignorance searched for it but couldn't find any. His silence upon being asked again about the certificate indicated his lack of preparedness for this final step.

The King was informed about Ignorance but, showing no inclination to meet him, commanded the two Shining Ones, who had guided Christian and Hopeful, to take Ignorance away. They bound him and carried him through the air to a door in the side of the hill, casting him into it. This act revealed a profound truth: there is a path to Hell even from the very gates of Heaven, just as there is from the city of Destruction.

With this startling realization, my dream ended, and I awoke to find that it was all a vision.

AFTER WORDS

Yet to all who did receive him, to those who believed in his name, he gave the right to become children of God—children born not of natural descent, nor of human decision or a husband's will, but born of God.

John 1:12-13

Maybe the journey of Pilgrim has struck a chord with you. Maybe you have felt God tugging at your heartstrings and you feel the need to respond. Perhaps you are now, like I was, hitting absolute bottom, feeling nothing but despair and desperation, having nowhere else to turn.

Now is your time to simply say, "Yes." To God.

Before you pray, I would like to offer a couple of words of encouragement. As Pilgrim discovered, it is not your words or actions that God is most interested in—it is your heart. We use words and actions to communicate our feelings and intent, but they are not what is of paramount importance.

Second, God makes things super simple for us—so simple that many find it hard to comprehend. Through the apostle, Paul, God says,

> *"If you confess with your mouth that Jesus is Lord and believe in your heart that God raised Him from the dead, you will be saved."*

That's it!

What is more, God *gives* us the faith to believe. Even in our struggles to grasp these concepts, God is right there alongside us. Not sure what to pray? You can make the following words your own right now.

> "Lord Jesus, for too long I've kept you out of my life. I know that I am a sinner and that I cannot save myself. No longer will I close the door when I hear you knocking. By faith, I gratefully receive your gift of salvation. I am ready to trust you as my Lord and Saviour. Thank you, Lord Jesus, for coming to earth. I believe you are the Son of God who died on the cross for my sins and rose from the dead. Thank you for bearing my sins and giving me the gift of eternal life. I believe your words are true. Come into my heart, Lord Jesus, and be my Savior. Amen[4]."

If you have prayed this prayer from the heart, congratulations! You are now a child of God!

---

[4] The word 'amen' is of Hebrew origin. In modern English it means 'so be it'. In Revelation 3:14, Jesus is referred to as, "the Amen, the faithful and true witness, the beginning of God's creation."

So that this special day will be remembered, you can record your commitment here:

Today, I invited Jesus to be my Lord and Saviour; I am Heaven bound!

This _____ day of _____, 20____

Signed _____

If you still have questions, you can contact the author here:

lookingintochoices@gmail.com

BY THE SAME AUTHOR

LEGEND:

(PB)   Available in paperback

(K)   Available in Kindle edition

(LP)   Available in Large Print paperback edition

(HC)   Available in Hard Cover

(R)   Public domain copyright restricts the distribution of this work to the following sovereign territories: Barbados, Belize, Bermuda, and Canada

For volume copies of any of these books (10+) or to contact the author, please send an email to dohauthor@gmail.com

The Pilgrim's Progress became one of the most published books in the English language, a testament to Bunyan's enduring influence as a writer and preacher. His life story, marked by adversity, faith, and creativity, remains a source of inspiration and a testament to the power of conviction and perseverance.

THE PILGRIM'S PROGRESS IN EVERYDAY ENGLISH (PB) (K) (LP) (HC) 144 pages. ISBN 979- 8872365181
In Canada — amazon.ca/dp/B0CQTLS2FY
In the USA — amazon.com/dp/B0CQTLS2FY
In the UK — amazon.co.uk/dp/B0CQTLS2FY

THE PILGRIM'S PROGRESS [EXCERPT]

CHAPTER 1 — THE CITY OF DESTRUCTION

While wandering in a wilderness of this world, I found a sheltered place to sleep. That night, I had a vivid dream. In it, I saw a man in ragged clothes, standing a short distance from his house, holding a *Book* and a heavy weight bearing down on him. The man opened the Book, and as he read, he started crying and shaking. Overwhelmed, he cried out, "What shall I do?"

The ragged man went back home, trying his best to hide his distress and anxiety from his family. But he couldn't keep his troubles to himself any longer. Finally, he confessed to his wife and children, "My dear family, I am in deep distress because of this heavy burden I carry. I'm sure that our  city will be destroyed by fire from Heaven, and we'll all be ruined unless we find a way to escape."

His family was stunned. They didn't really believe his fears, thinking that he was having a mental breakdown. Evening approached and they hoped sleep would calm him, so they hurriedly put him to bed. But he had a restless night, filled with sighs and tears. In the morning, he said he felt even worse and tried to talk to them again, but they became cold and harsh with him, thinking he was going insane.

Feeling isolated, he spent his time alone, praying for his family and seeking comfort for himself. He walked the streets near his house, sometimes reading, sometimes praying. He continued like this for several days.

When I first read Mere Christianity, I couldn't help but wonder if the average North American reader could fully grasp the essence of this book without an English-to-"English" dictionary at their side. Even I, though born and raised in England, found myself Googling the meaning of some of Lewis's colloquialisms from the 1940s. Lewis himself acknowledges the shifting nature of language and word usage over time. Many readers have appreciated this everyday English version.

MERE CHRISTIANITY IN EVERYDAY ENGLISH (PB) (K) (LP) (R)
190 pages. ISBN 979-8396258051
In Canada – amazon.ca/dp/B0C6BR61WJ

Chapter 1 - The Law of Human Nature [Excerpt]

Everyone has heard folks quarrelling. Sometimes it sounds funny, sometimes it's simply unpleasant; but regardless of how it sounds, I believe we can glean something quite significant from listening to what they're saying. They'll say things like: "How'd you like it if someone did the same to you?" — "That's my seat, I was here first" — "Leave him be, he's not bothering you" — "Why should you be the first to barge in?" — "Give me a piece of your orange, I gave you a piece of mine" — "Come on, you promised." Every day, people utter such phrases, the educated and the uneducated, children and adults alike.

What piques my interest about these remarks is that the individual making them isn't just stating their displeasure with the other's behaviour. They're invoking a certain standard of behaviour that they expect the other to recognise. The other person rarely retorts: "To hell with your standard." They'll usually attempt to argue that their actions don't really contradict the standard, or if they do, there's a special exception. They'll pretend there's a specific reason in this particular instance that the person who nabbed the seat first should not keep it, or that things were completely different when they were handed a piece of orange, or that an unexpected event exempts them from keeping their promise.

It appears, in fact, as though both parties are mindful of some sort of Law or Rule concerning fair play, decent behaviour, morality, or whatever else you want to call it, about which they genuinely concur. And they do. If they didn't, they might resort to animalistic fighting, but they wouldn't be able to quarrel in the distinctly human sense. Quarrelling entails attempting to demonstrate that the other person is in the wrong. This endeavour would make no sense unless you and they had some sort of consensus on what constitutes Right and Wrong, just like

Lewis himself makes reference to the changes in language and word usage over time. This led me to rework his book into MERE CHRISTIANITY in Everyday English. Never did I expect such a positive response to my efforts, with an eighty percent five-star rating on Amazon. This success has led me to tackle THE SCREWTAPE LETTERS which Lewis had written in the year before Mere Christianity. It is hoped that The Screwtape Letters in Everyday English will likewise enable it to be enjoyed by a broader audience.

THE SCREWTAPE LETTERS IN EVERYDAY ENGLISH (PB) (K) (R)
An Easy-to-Read Version of C.S. Lewis' Literary Classic
190 pages. In Canada — amazon.ca/dp/B0CT8QG1XF

The Screwtape Letters [Excerpt]
Letter 1

Dear Wormwood,

I've taken note of your efforts to influence your subject's reading choices and to keep him close to his atheist friends. But aren't you being a bit naive? You seem to believe that arguing with him is the best way to keep him from God's influence. This might've been effective a few hundred years ago. Back then, people had a clear sense of what was true or not; and if they believed something, they acted on it. They connected their thoughts with their actions and changed their behavior based on logic. However, with the influence of media and other factors, we've mostly changed that. From a young age, your subject has been exposed to multiple conflicting philosophies. He doesn't see ideas as "right" or "wrong," but more like "academic" or "practical," "outdated" or "modern," "traditional" or "cutthroat." Buzzwords, not logic, are your best tools to steer him away from the Church. Don't waste your time trying to convince him that atheism is the truth. Just make him feel it's bold, modern, or brave — that it's the way of the future. That's what he'll care about.

The problem with arguing is that you're playing into God's hands. He's a good debater too. And by engaging in argument, you risk awakening your subject's rational mind. Once that happens, anything can follow. Even if you manage to steer his thoughts in our favor, you're strengthening his habit of considering the big picture, pulling him away from the fleeting distractions of daily life. Your job is to keep him focused on the superficial; make him consider that to be the "real life." Don't let him ponder too deeply on what "real" means.

IS JESUS GOD? WHAT THE BIBLE TEACHES US (PB) (K) (LP)
AUTHORED BY DAVID HARRISON AND BERND FLOCK
113 pages. ISBN: 979-8401914781
In Canada — amazon.ca/dp/B09QF44Z26
In the USA — amazon.com/dp/B09QF44Z26
In the UK — amazon.co.uk/dp/B09QF44Z26

INTRODUCTION - IS JESUS GOD? [EXCERPT]

This devotional book may help you answer the age-old question: Is Jesus God? Here, we rely totally on Scripture for the answers, both from the Old and New Testaments.

Hindus believe Jesus is just one of thousands of gods, Jehovah Witnesses believe that Jesus was a god, Muslims believe that Jesus was a great prophet. While there is no clear consensus on what Jews believe about Jesus there is general agreement about what they do not believe, especially about Jesus as Messiah. Yet the Bible, read comprehensively, teaches that Jesus was fully God *and* Messiah – even in his humanity.

Many people say: "He is God himself" but can we really say that? How can he be God when there are so many verses that show that he is under the Father or separate from the Father? Does the Bible teach about a triune God? Is it at all important that Jesus is God? Many ask why God didn't make it clear in His word. Pascal, a Catholic theologian, reasoned:

> "Because He wanted to appear unveiled to those who seek him with all their heart, and because he wanted to stay veiled to those who flee from him with all their heart, he set his recognisability in such a way, that he gave signs of Himself, visible to those who seek him but invisible to those who do not seek him. There is enough light for those who want nothing else but to see, and there is enough darkness for the others who don't want to see."

If Jesus is God, then we have to give him the worship that God should have; to neglect in giving him this would be an insult to God. If Jesus Christ isn't God, then our worship would be blasphemy and idolatry, even if he was a higher being. If Jesus isn't God, then many are sinning because they *"worshiped and served the creature more than the Creator, who is blessed forever"* Romans 1:25.

THRIVE! TURNING THE CHURCH RIGHT-SIDE UP
190 Pages. ISBN 9798882973864
In Canada — amazon.ca/dp/B0CXM2WTWK
In the USA — amazon.com/dp/B0CXM2WTWK
In the UK — amazon.co.uk/dp/B0CXM2WTWK

Group Study Edition ISBN: 9798321137420

THRIVE! [EXCERPT]

INTRODUCTION – THRIVING

An older woman who has recently started attending our church explained her reason for leaving her former fellowship. She said, "There have been many reasons, but when they started serving lemonade and stopped serving coffee due to lack of resources, well, that was the final straw."

Everyone has a breaking point, but her statement revealed to me that her old church had failed to thrive. It may seem trivial – almost humorous if it weren't so tragic – that the choice of lemonade or coffee should have been her ultimate breaking point, the straw that broke the camel's back. What were the potential myriad reasons underlying that 'final straw'?

Many books have been written on ways to attract people into the Church and help them find God, but they do not focus on the underlying causes of failure to thrive or the countless promises of God on how to thrive. Without a firm foundation, all the programs in the world will not bring to life the Church God intended. This book focuses its attention on creating a foundation for perpetual thriving.

I want this to be a Book of Encouragement, not a Book of Condemnation. The opposite of 'failure to thrive' is excitingly described by Dr. Luke:

> *"Every day they continued to meet together in the temple courts. They broke bread in their homes and ate together with glad and sincere hearts, praising God and enjoying the favour of all the people. And the Lord added to their number daily those who were being saved." Acts 2:46-47*

Whether Hindu, Jew, Jehovah's Witness, Christian (Protestant, Orthodox, Coptic or Catholic), Mormon, Sikh, Muslim, Buddhist, Bahá'í, Shinto, Unitarian, New Age, Atheist or agnostic, this book will provide you with a path of reason and logical understanding so that you can find true inner peace and have absolute confidence of what lies ahead without anxiety!

WHAT'S NEXT? (PB) (K)

In Canada — amazon.ca/dp/B0CXY38T2Z
In the USA — amazon.com/dp/B0CXY38T2Z
In the UK — amazon.co.uk/dp/B0CXY38T2Z

A Group Study version is also available. An excellent follow-up resource to the Alpha Course®, outreach, prison ministry, etc. ISBN 9798884327054

What's Next? [Excerpt]

Chapter 1 — What's Next and the Fragility of Life

The following story was related to me firsthand by a young motorcycle rider, while filling up at the gas station where he worked.

You have a passion for motorbikes. For three years you've worked hard and saved to buy your first new bike. Despite your youth, you are a cautious rider and don't take unnecessary chances. You even have a Go-Pro camera on your helmet to keep a record of your motorcycling activity. Suddenly, the driver in front of you slams on her brakes (a distracted driver on her phone). You react immediately and squeeze the brakes with all your strength. The front brake grabs a fraction of a second before the rear brake, causing the bike to go end-over-end into the back of the car. You go flying high into the air and land on the hood of the woman's vehicle — your mangled motorbike lying in her back seat. Amazingly, you walk away. The woman is charged with careless driving and the insurance company pays for a new bike. A while later you are driving along the highway, another motorcycle comes up behind and somehow clips you. Again, you survive, but this time with a broken arm and four broken ribs. The paramedics are amazed that you are alive.

The metaphorical dice of fate have been rolled; it seems you've won. Or have you? That depends.

You are a Russian soldier driving along a dusty dirt road somewhere near the front line in Ukraine. Three kilometres away a Javelin anti-tank missile with its nineteen-pound warhead has just been launched and is heading straight for you. In a matter of seconds your tank, with you in it, is about to be engulfed in a fiery explosion. The odds of this happening to you in Ukraine is about one in two hundred on any given day. That's the unpredictable existence, or the abrupt cessation thereof, for a Russian tank driver.

The metaphorical dice of fate have been rolled; it seems you've lost. Or have you? That depends.

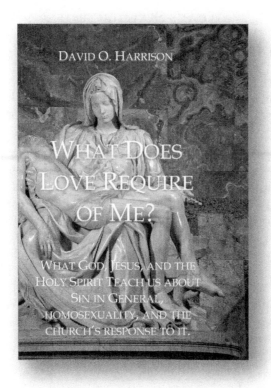

In this book, WHAT DOES LOVE REQUIRE OF ME? David strives to find what God, Jesus, and the Holy Spirit would convey to us about sin in general, the topic of homosexuality in particular, and how church leaders should be handling these topics with their congregations. An extraordinarily challenging task in these prophetic times.

WHAT DOES LOVE REQUIRE OF ME (PB) (K)

200 pages. ISBN No. 9798767554140
Canada — amazon.ca/dp/B09LWFLFW3
USA — amazon.com/dp/B09LWFLFW3
In the UK — amazon.co.uk/dp/B09LWFLFW3

What Does Love Require of Me?

Introduction

In his book, *God's Final Word – Understanding Revelation*, author Ray C. Stedman gives an excellent outline of Jesus' words to the Seven Churches, noting that the church in Pergamum, at the time, was "flirting with corruption and immorality." He conjectures that many of today's church congregations 'flirt with immorality', opening their arms to everyone in the name of acceptance and inclusivity, tolerating in their midst that which God calls "an abomination" – not at all referring exclusively to active homosexuality.

A crucial question we need to ask ourselves is, "Am I, or is our church or denomination, deliberately or misguidedly, flirting with immorality?" If the answer is "Yes", how should we expect God to react – His rebuke and discipline, 'spitting us out of His mouth' or something else?

Conversely, we need to ask ourselves, "How are we going to attract, and offer a sense of belonging, to those who are in need of repair, to those who Jesus instructs us, "...*go and make disciples of all nations* (the LGBTQ community included), *baptizing them in the name of the Father and of the Son and of the Holy Spirit, and teaching them to obey everything I have commanded you.*"?

I recently read the book *Irresistible: Reclaiming the New that Jesus Unleashed for the World* by Pastor Andy Stanley. In this must-read book, Andy asks the question, "What does love require of me?" It is a question that has been haunting me since the moment I read it.

The most fundamental question of our time must be, "Why do I believe what I believe?" One must ask oneself, "Is what I believe based on truth and logic, or is what I believe based on ignorance of facts, emotion and relativity?" Why do you believe what you believe?

In this book, David Harrison argues that a lack of knowledge of God is mostly based on wilful ignorance, a failure to thoroughly investigate the reality of God. Obviously, one cannot prove a negative, the argument that there is no God. Conversely, one can argue that God does exist and provide rational proof of His existence.

IF GOD THEN... THE LOGICAL GOD (PB) (K)
GOD   429 pages. ISBN 9798357310927
In Canada — amazon.ca/dp/B0BHV3VX7V
In the USA — amazon.com/dp/B0BHV3VX7V
In the UK — amazon.co.uk/dp/B0BHV3VX7V

If God, Then... [Excerpt]

Chapter 0 — All Journeys Have a Beginning

While I have included personal experiences to illustrate the intimacy of the God I so cherish, one of the main objectives of this book is to focus on the third point of reference, the God we see in nature. The God *everyone* can see—if they so wish.

In trying to ensure that I do not err by making egregious errors in logic or hiding falsehoods in the arguments I present, I approached a self-described atheist, Barry Goldberg, to see if he would review a draft copy and highlight any mistakes in reasoning I might have made. He declined to conduct a review, but he kindly sent me a list of pitfalls to avoid and definitions that need to be clearly articulated:

- Do not present logical arguments divorced from actual evidence.

- Do not define terms to your advantage.

- Make the proper assumptions (I have endeavoured to avoid assumptions altogether).

- Avoid carefully chosen definitions and assumptions that may or may not be warranted.

- Be noticeably clear, up front, exactly what your definition of "God" is.

- If you cannot connect the dots between whatever "God" you think you can prove and any actual deity worshiped by anybody throughout history (*i.e.*, a deity anybody cares about), then be upfront about that fact as well so people do not get disappointed when they get to the end and think you have moved the goalposts on them.

Barry concluded, "It might not be as exciting as being the first person in 2000 years to prove that the Christian God exists, but you will at least get points for being honest about your claims." The first person in 2000 years? I do love a challenge!